MW00830424

THE **XANDER KING** SERIES

SCOURGE

ALSO BY BRADLEY WRIGHT

SCOURGE

Copyright © 2018 by **Bradley Wright**

All rights reserved. No part of this publication may be reproduced, distributed or transmitted in any form or by any means, without prior written permission.

Bradley Wright/King's Ransom Books
www.bradleywrightauthor.com

Publisher's Note: This is a work of fiction. Names, characters, places, and incidents are a product of the author's imagination. Locales and public names are sometimes used for atmospheric purposes. Any resemblance to actual people, living or dead,
or to businesses, companies, events, institutions, or locales is completely coincidental.
Cover Design by DDD, Deranged Doctor Designs
SCOURGE/ Bradley Wright. -- 1st ed.
ISBN - 978-0-9973926-5-4

For Kyle Hamilton
#BFFFEBBBHMMDD

Throughout the history of our young nation, we have seen our military go bravely into battle, armed with courage and willing to make the ultimate sacrifice.

— John M. McHugh

Technology is a useful slave but a dangerous master.

— Christian Lous Lange

SCOURGE: /skurj/
noun

1. a person or thing that causes great trouble or suffering.
2. a group of mosquitos.

SCOURGE

1

Change the World

"THIS WILL CHANGE THE WORLD FOREVER."

A frail man in a white lab coat pushed a pair of black-rimmed glasses up the bridge of his nose as he extended his hand toward Gregor. In the palm of his hand sat a small stainless steel box.

Gregor Maragos gave Doctor Birschbach, the scientist he hired over five years ago, a contemplative look. Tens of millions of dollars had been spent on Birschbach and his team of experts just so he could hear those six words. Now that he had heard them, Gregor didn't know how to react. If Birschbach's claim was true, then he had just mastered nanotechnology. And if he had in fact just mastered nanotechnology, the entire world would be at Gregor Maragos's mercy. So, before celebration, he had to be sure.

"Change the world . . . how?" Gregor asked, void of emotion.

A wry smile grew across the German scientist's face. "Mr. Maragos, it will change the world in whatever way you see fit."

Gregor turned his eyes from Birschbach's mouth to the box. In a nervous twitch, he smoothed the thinning dark hair that was tousled atop his head. Gregor wasn't a tall man, not in great shape either. As usual, he looked disheveled. He always had better things to do with his time than worry about his appearance.

Gregor's father, however, had been quite the opposite. Gregor was nothing like him. All of his father's hard-earned billions had made his father a world-renowned and highly revered man. Gregor longed for that, but he wasn't built for it. He hadn't the personality nor the appearance. Since his father's death, Gregor's brother, Andonios, had stepped into his father's spotlight. He was the face of his father's business and a world-traveling playboy. "A modern-day Greek god," the tabloids called him. But this, the contents of this shiny little box, would finally bring *Gregor* into the spotlight. More than that, it would shadow his father's and his brother's accomplishments like the moon moving across the sun in a total eclipse. He would have far more than just money and influence—he would have absolute power.

Gregor carefully took the box from Birschbach's hand. "You have tested this?"

"Of course, Gregor."

"It is free of any glitches?"

"It is flawless."

"You're certain?" Gregor was adamant.

"Yes, I am 100 percent certain."

"And your team, they can replicate this?"

"Of course," Birschbach said, eyeing his achievement with great pride. "We have enough materials to produce millions of them."

"How long?"

"How long what, Gregor?"

"To produce these millions."

"N-not long. But, sir, you must be *very* careful with this—"

"Call them over," Gregor interrupted. He unbuttoned the black jacket of his worn and faded three-piece suit. The only suit he owned, and he had all but worn it out.

"I'm sorry?" Birschbach looked nervous.

"Your team, call all of them over here. I want to make an announcement."

Birschbach turned to his assistant, and his assistant then announced to the fifteen men and women working diligently in the large laboratory behind them to gather around.

Birschbach smiled at Gregor, and Gregor simply nodded his head. Once the men and women surrounded them, Gregor cleared his throat and once again attempted to smooth back his hair.

"Doctor Birschbach has informed me that we have just made history."

The men and women smiled and congratulated themselves with a hearty round of applause. Gregor himself was not amused.

"He also informed me that you will be able to reproduce what I am holding in my hand more than a million times over. When I asked him how long it would take to do this, instead of answering the question, he was about to warn me. Doctor Birschbach, would you like to finish what you were about to tell me?"

Birschbach's smile held trepidation. "Certainly." He turned toward his team, his back to Gregor. "What I was going to warn Mr. Maragos of is something you all know very well."

Gregor reached inside his suit jacket, pulled out a vintage black Luger P08 pistol, pressed it firmly against the back of Birschbach's head, and squeezed the trigger.

In shock after watching their boss and mentor's brains be blown out through his forehead, Birschbach's team of some of the world's most renowned scientists regarded Gregor in fear as he tucked the pistol back inside his jacket. But no one said a word.

"I want you to remember the feeling of fear you all have right now." Gregor gave a sweeping look at the men and women that cowered in front of him. "Understand that if I ask you a question, you answer it. If I want a warning, I will ask for one. Is that clear?"

The frightened men and women nodded without hesitation.

"Who is in charge of this operation now that the great Doctor Birschbach is no longer able to fulfill his duties?"

A short woman, midforties, short dark hair with lightning white streaks and a warrior's expression, stepped forward confidently. "I am."

"And you are?" Gregor asked.

"Doctor Emelia Kruger. And it will take three days to produce a thousand bots. Once the manufacturing quirks are streamlined, I can have an additional five hundred thousand in the following week. Going any faster would produce an inferior product. And I will not disrespect you by doing so."

Gregor smiled. A crooked, pleased, and sinister smile. "Very well. I will not interrupt your work again. Proceed."

"Shall I have someone clean this up?" Dr. Kruger asked Gregor, motioning toward her fallen colleague.

"That won't be necessary," he told her. "I've hired a new security team. They will handle Dr. Birschbach as well."

Dr. Kruger glanced down at the box in Gregor's hand. "Would you like a demonstration, Mr. Maragos?"

"Nothing would please me more."

Dr. Kruger smiled. "Prepare to be amazed."

2

The Italian Job

NIGHT HAD FALLEN OVER VENICE, Italy. A warm breeze from the lagoon flooded Piazza San Marco, and so too did the pleasant notes of the four-piece ensemble playing for the crowd of diners at the north end. The piazza was filled with lovers sharing wine and vacationers sharing dinner. History, culture, romance, and everything else you would expect to find in a unique and centuries-old city surrounded—engulfed—everyone in the square.

Everyone except for Xander King.

Normally while in Italy, the twenty-nine-year-old would be enjoying his surroundings just like everyone else. More than everyone else, in fact. He had the money, the looks, and the charisma to tear through the city and the countryside alike, chasing beautiful women, imbibing every detail of Italian culture, thriving in its carefree, come-what-may environment.

His six-foot-three-inch muscular frame served as the perfect vehicle for a successful young businessman in the most romantic city in the world.

However, that muscular frame, these days, was being used far more for the things that it had been trained to do as a Navy SEAL. This night would be anything but carefree, and if there was a chance for romance, it was going to have to come much later. As Xander took a sip of his Chianti, his focus wasn't on Piazza San Marco as a whole but rather on one man in particular. A well-known assassin named Alessio Brancati.

"Stop staring at the woman in the red dress and focus on Brancati," Sam told Xander through his earpiece.

Samantha Harrison, former MI6 agent in London, now the fierce backbone to Xander's clandestine CIA unit called Reign, was lurking somewhere in the shadows of the square. As usual, ribbing Xander as she simultaneously searched the nooks and crannies of the square, making certain that Brancati was working alone.

"I wasn't looking at the woman in the red dress. But I am now. Aren't you supposed to keep me focused?"

"Though it shouldn't be, that does seem to be a big part of my job."

"You're failing miserably," Xander said.

Sam had always been a hard-ass. But lately she had been in a particularly foul mood due to the ending of her romance with Xander's closest friend, Kyle. Kyle would normally be along for the ride as a member of Reign, but the CIA finally forced him into getting formal training, so he was spending a few weeks at Camp Peary. He and Sam had decided it best if they went back to just being friends. It was a mutual decision between them, but somehow Xander was still feeling the ill effects of the newly single Brit. Her legendary crabbiness was reaching new heights every day.

"Bugger off, would you?" Sam said. "Looks like Brancati and Red Dress are on the move."

Xander finished his glass of wine and stood from his table in the back of the square. "I'm a little hurt, Sam."

Sam knew exactly where Xander was headed. "Save it. I don't care how debonair you think you look in your tuxedo."

You spend enough time with someone, you know what they'll say before they say it. Xander and Sam had been fighting alongside each other long enough to know all that and more. No other pair worked better together, but Xander's favorite part about his time with Sam was giving her all the hell she could handle along the way.

Xander smiled. "That means you know I look good. Thanks, Sam." Xander heard Sam sigh as he rounded the last of the tables, following Brancati and his date from a distance.

CIA Director Mary Hartsfield handled Reign exclusively, though it was really Sam who ran the operation. The CIA had been trying to bring Xander back into service, and his only stipulation for coming back was that there were no stipulations. His team had carte blanche. The only unit within any of the government acronyms to have such freedom.

A day ago, Director Hartsfield had sent photos of Brancati and his presumed location. The intel from Italian intelligence—AISI—was that Brancati had surfaced in Venice two nights ago, checking into his hotel under a different name, Lorenzo Russo. The reason the CIA cared was because Brancati had been involved in a failed CIA mission in London, which resulted in an agent's death. He supposedly interfered with the now-dead CIA agent as she attempted to pass along some top secret information that she had acquired while tapping a phone conversation of a US citizen working in Greece. The agent was attempting to hand off a flash drive with a recording of the conversation. A conversation that supposedly held global implications. Brancati was hired—by whom the CIA wasn't sure—to acquire the flash drive, but apparently the information was important enough that killing a CIA agent was necessary. This was a sure-fire way to have the world's best defense after you, which is why Xander and Sam were now breathing down Brancati's neck.

"There are no signs he has help," Sam said, "which isn't a surprise. Most assassins work alone."

Xander was now in the middle of the square. Brancati and his date were walking toward the Museo Correr at the south side of the square, opposite Saint Mark's Basilica. Xander wasn't much of a museum guy. Chasing bad guys tends to get in the way of enjoying local culture. However, he had visited Venice enough to know that Museo Correr housed a collection of works that displayed the art and history of Venice, one of his favorite cities. On this night, however, the ballroom had been converted into a modern art gallery, and some of the world's wealthiest collectors had been invited to bid on some of the work. Several of the pieces were extremely rare, which brought the hobnobbingest of hobnobbers to Venice. Even many Italian socialites who weren't collectors received invites, one's net worth being the only consideration. Which is why Xander received an invite, even though his interests couldn't lie further from an old painting hanging on a wall.

"Do I really have to go in here?" Xander asked.

"These are *your* people, Xander. They don't care that you're just a simple Kentucky boy. Your money spends all the same."

The money Sam spoke of was the fortune Xander's father left behind when he and his mother were murdered when Xander was a teenager. And though his father turned out to be anything but the man Xander thought he was, people in these circles only cared if the money was in the bank, not how it got there. And while some knew and respected the fact that Xander chose to serve his country in the Navy, most had no clue. They were only aware of what he'd done with the money: his bourbon company and prized racehorses. This was fine by him; it made it easier to move amongst them in his current capacity, the agent who would die to keep his country safe.

Xander scoffed. "These high-society snobs are not *my* people, Sammy. You're just jealous because you wanted to go to this thing with me."

"Just don't let Brancati hand off the flash drive without you seeing it. A flip of the hair from the right woman and you might lose track of Brancati entirely."

A new voice spoke up in Xander's and Sam's ears. An older man with a strong country accent. "Do the two o' you ever quit? It's like I'm listenin' to an old married couple argue over the TV remote."

Jack Bronson was another unlikely member of Reign. Once retired, the old veteran of the CIA was brought back into the fold the year before and had ended up being an invaluable member of the team. Jack was like a real-life cowboy, and he and Xander had hit it off immediately. When Xander began Reign, Jack was happy to come in off the ranch and get back into the action. His sniper skills had saved Xander and crew on more than one occasion.

Neither Sam nor Xander acknowledged Jack's comment. Brancati and his date were at the entrance of the museum. Xander let a few more attendees fall in behind Brancati before he pulled his invitation from his lapel pocket and approached the door.

Sam brought things back to business. "All right. We haven't a clue if Brancati has the flash drive on his person. He may well already be rid of it. So just hold back and observe, Xander. There may be a drop, or he may be here on assignment to take someone out. Or he might be in the mood to buy a painting. Let's just be patient and let him do his thing. We aren't here to keep him from killing someone, so don't be a hero. The flash drive's location is far more valuable."

"Are you at his hotel yet?" Xander asked.

"Almost," Sam said. "I should have plenty of time to search Brancati's room. I'll let you know what I find, and you let me know if he leaves."

"Got it," Xander said. "Jack, watch her back."

"Roger that."

3

A Night at the Museum

XANDER HANDED the doorman his invitation.

"Mr. King, so nice of you to join us."

Xander nodded and entered the ballroom. He was greeted with a glass of champagne and an eyeful of quintessential Venetian decor. The massive room had magnificent vaulted ceilings covered in murals as well as golden accents, propped up on large white stone columns, all around the room. The walls displayed what Xander figured were considered brilliant works of art, something he would have to leave to the professionals. It was the sea of people wandering the room that fell more into Xander's expertise. He watched as Brancati ushered the woman in the red dress through the crowd. The way he interacted with her suggested they weren't all that familiar. Instead of holding her hand or directing her at the small of her back, he gripped informally at the back of her elbow. The way he walked with purpose, not stopping to admire a single painting, told Xander he wasn't here for the artwork, but that came as no surprise.

Brancati seemed to know exactly where he was going. Xander continued to follow as Brancati made his way to the back of the room. There was a painting set apart from the rest. It looked like a three-year-old had scribbled in bright colors on a large canvas. But the way people were ogling it, Xander knew it must be considered the crown jewel. He watched as Brancati approached a man and woman who were busy admiring the painting.

Sam updated Xander in his ear. "All right, I'm in Brancati's room. It looks quite bare, but I'll give it a go."

Xander pretended to enjoy the painting closest to where Brancati was now greeting the couple. Out of the corner of his eye he could see that the man Brancati shook hands with was in his midthirties, olive skin, well-manicured dark hair, wearing a navy-blue tuxedo, presumably stitched by the finest of custom tailors. The woman beside him, at least as far as Xander could see, was a knockout. Her long blond hair hid most of her face from Xander's point of view, but her beautiful curves couldn't be hidden from anyone in that long, light-pink, form-fitting evening gown.

Sam's comment about Xander being distracted by women ran through his mind, and he quickly refocused on the two men having a conversation. The two ladies didn't interact whatsoever. In fact, Red Dress scanned the room as if she was looking for someone. Something didn't feel right. When her sweep of the room came to his corner, Xander stepped behind a large man and turned his back to her.

Xander bent down to fake tie his shoe. "Sam, any information on Red Dress? Something is off."

"We have no information on her. This is the first time Brancati has been seen with her."

"Something's not right," he repeated as he rose from his crouched position.

Alarm bells were going off in Xander's head. He hadn't noticed anything strange out in the square, but considering the way Brancati and his date were clearly not romantic, coupled with the odd way Red Dress had scanned the room, the sensation that they were working together pulsed in Xander's lizard brain. He gave a quick side glance, and this time Red Dress was gone. He gave the room a casual once-over but didn't see any sign of her. When he looked back to Brancati, he was wrapping up his conversation with a handshake.

The handshake lingered longer than it should have.

The olive-skinned man immediately moved his hand from Brancati's to his pocket, sliding something inside.

"I've got eyes on the flash drive."

Xander said this a little too loud.

The large man he was hiding behind turned to face him. "Excuse me?"

Xander smiled, then glanced at the champagne glass in his own hand. "Sorry, I'm a lightweight."

The large man gave Xander a pitying look. Xander looked over his shoulder, and Brancati was walking away.

Before he could let Sam know Brancati was leaving, her voice came back in his ear. The hint of panic in her tone sent a chill down his spine. "Xander, the only thing in Brancati's room is a folder. And the only thing in it are pictures of you. Get the hell out of there, NOW!"

A lot of things bounced through Xander's mind in that moment, but he didn't have time to process any of them. As if his mind wasn't jumbled enough, when he looked up again at the olive-skinned man, whom he now believed had the flash drive, the identity of the gorgeous blonde on his arm finally revealed itself, and it nearly took his breath away.

Sarah Gilbright.

Sarah was the CIA agent tasked with following Xander last year. She then fought by his side as she helped him find out who murdered his parents. And she was the woman who once shared his bed and still held a very special place in his heart. Sam had told Xander that Sarah couldn't be a part of Reign because she had already been reassigned elsewhere. This olive-skinned man must be her assignment.

Just as Xander's processor whirred back to life after the shock of seeing Sarah there, and he remembered what Sam had just told him, Sarah looked up, and the two of them locked eyes. Her mouth actually gaped open. Her look of shock mirrored Xander's, and for a moment neither of them moved.

"Xander," Sam said in his ear, "are you safe? Did you get out of there?"

Sam's words snapped him out of his trance, and it was none too soon. Xander glanced to his left and barely got his right arm up in time to block the syringe in Red Dress's hand. She must have seen him in her sweep of the room. Xander's sense that they were working together had been dead on. Red Dress wasn't expecting Xander to react so quickly, and it showed on her face as he grabbed her wrist holding the syringe and turned it toward the ceiling. A black heart tattoo at the base of her thumb stared back at him. At the same time, he wrenched his hips to the right and hit her with a left hook to the kidney so hard that everyone in the room heard her scream.

With her wrist still in his grip, Xander glanced around the room for Brancati but couldn't find him. Xander felt vulnerable in the crowd. He needed to tip the scales more in his favor, and fast. Brancati wasn't the type of assassin you wanted to leave an opening for. Red Dress was trying to regain her composure, but she'd likely never been hit like that before. Xander took the syringe from her hand, threw it on the ground, and stomped on it. He grabbed a silver tray of champagne glasses from a waiter nearby, turned it in his hand, and smashed Red Dress over the head. She slumped in a heap onto the ballroom floor.

"Red Dress is down but not out," Xander announced to his

team listening in his ear. "Zhanna, if you're close, bring a police officer and have her arrested. We need to talk to someone, and I have a feeling Brancati won't be breathing long enough to interrogate him."

Zhanna was the fifth member of the six-person Reign team. Zhanna, former KGB in Russia, came along for the ride when Xander went after mafia boss Vitalii Dragov in Moscow—who also turned out to be her estranged father. She was so grateful for Xander's help that she wanted to continue fighting alongside him and the rest of his ragtag team.

"I'm on it, be there in five," Zhanna replied.

Xander looked at the waiter. "You saw what happened, right?"

The waiter nodded. "Yeah, mate, she tried to bloody stick you with that needle. Then you took that bitch down!"

"Right. Mind waiting here and telling the police that? I've gotta run."

"Sure, mate, do your thing."

Xander scanned the room that was now emptying quickly after the commotion. He didn't see any sign of Brancati, nor could he find Sarah and her boyfriend, Mr. Flash Drive. Xander was vulnerable. He had only his knife, no gun. He needed to get out of the open spaces of the ballroom and into the alleys that ran along the canals. He stayed low as he moved amongst the crowd. As he approached the exit of the museum, everyone was moving in the same direction, except up ahead two individuals were moving upstream. They were either Zhanna and the policeman or two of Brancati's men coming for him.

"Almost to the museum, Xander. Hold tight," Zhanna said in his ear.

So much for Brancati the assassin working solo.

4

A Knife in a Gunfight

XANDER CROUCHED a little lower and began to walk backward into the crowd, away from his oncoming enemies.

"Two inside that I know of, Zhanna," Xander said. "Sam, are you close?"

"Jack and I are entering the north end of the square," Sam replied. "Be to you in seconds. Do you have eyes on Brancati?"

"I got distracted."

"The woman, I'm sure."

"Predictable, I know," Xander said. "I have to find another way out. The main entrance is blocked."

"Across from the fourth chandelier, farthest away from the main entrance, there is a service door. Through the kitchen, then you'll find an alley."

Xander's eyes followed Sam's directions. "Got it."

"Meet you there."

Xander moved through the last of the crowd to the door Sam mentioned. He didn't have to ask how she knew about it. He knew she had studied the plans for the building in preparation. There wasn't much his partner in crime missed. The door was unlocked, and there was a short hallway that led to a swinging door. The door swung inward to the kitchen, and a man hurried in, but it wasn't a waiter. It was a man dressed in all black, undoubtedly now staring at exactly what or whom he was looking for.

Xander slipped his hand inside his tuxedo jacket and gripped the Micarta inlay on the handle of his Chris Reeve Sebenza 21 tactical knife. Before heading to Camp Peary, his friend Kyle had tried to talk him into something more John Wick, but Xander preferred the strength of the Idaho-made blade over the sexy stylings of an inferior Hollywood-style knife. The man in black standing ten feet in front of him in the narrow hallway reached into his pocket and pulled out a blade of his own.

"Been a while since I've been in a knife fight," Xander said in jest.

The tall and wiry Italian-looking man uttered something Xander couldn't translate, and rushed toward him. Xander pulled his knife, flipped the blade from the handle with his thumb, and waited patiently for the man to arrive.

"I've got company near the kitchen," Xander announced to the team. "I'm gonna be a few seconds late."

The man lunged at Xander, thrusting his knife forward. Xander bounced backward on the balls of his feet, escaping the man's blade. The man moved in again with no variation in his attack, so this time when he thrust his blade forward, Xander met it with the tip of his patent leather oxford, sending the man's knife clanking against the wall. The man rushed to pick it up, but when he bent over, his leg was exposed. Xander wheeled a Thai kick down hard on the back of the man's knee. It buckled beneath him, spinning him around and landing him on his back. The man looked up at Xander. To avoid being sprayed with blood, Xander attacked the man's stomach instead of his neck. Three lightning-fast strikes and Xander was able to move on without worry the man would come for him later.

Before Xander could open the swinging door to the kitchen, he heard gunshots just outside.

Sam.

Xander kept his knife in hand and bulldozed the door, sprinting around the service tables in the middle of the kitchen.

"This is coordinated, Xander. We must divert from the alley beyond the kitchen. There is a gunman there. Are you good on your own?"

"Just find Brancati," Xander said as he pushed open the door to the alley.

The gunman Sam mentioned now stood right in front of Xander. The short and stalky man went to raise his gun, but Xander was close enough to punch down on the man's hand, sending the gun clacking to the cobblestone below. Xander front-kicked him in the solar plexus, forcing him to stumble back; then Xander took two steps forward and thrust his knife into the same spot he'd just kicked, then pulled the blade free. When the man grabbed at the wound in his stomach, Xander jabbed his knife into the man's throat. The man fell to his back. As Xander glanced down the dimly lit street, two men rounded the corner in a rush. Xander knew they were coming for him.

Where is Brancati?

Xander stepped back to pick up the man's gun, but the two men were already firing on him and he couldn't risk it. He turned left and began to sprint.

"Get down! Everyone get down!" Xander shouted as he ran. Bystanders were cowering, their hands over their heads, and he kept screaming, "Stay down!"

Xander knew up ahead on the left there was a walkway back into the main square. There was a good chance more men were waiting there, and with only a knife in hand, he couldn't afford to run across more armed gunmen than were already chasing him. Beyond that walkway, straight in front of him, he knew the canal awaited. He wasn't sure, but he thought there was a connection to the walkway that ran along the lagoon just across the narrow turn of the canal.

"Where the hell is everyone?" Xander shouted to his team. Just ahead of him was the canal. Under the yellow glow of lights hanging from adjacent buildings, he could just make out two gondolas at the edge. Several people were boarding them for a romantic float through the streets of water. Sarah flashed in his mind again. He couldn't for the life of him fathom what she was doing there. But she would have to wait. Xander heard gunshots, both in his ear and just on the other side of the building he was running along.

"Pinned down in the square," Sam said.

Zhanna chimed in, "Just took down two men in museum."

"I've got two on my tail, with guns," Xander said. "I'm running along the street behind you toward the canal. Don't worry about me. Just find Brancati!"

Xander heard gunshots behind him. The two men were closing in. There was no time to slow down. Xander approached the people boarding the gondolas. As he ran, he found a small hole in between them; then beyond them he registered the court-yard that led to the walkway along the port.

"Get down!" Xander shouted.

There was a stone rail about ten feet away across the water. As he squeezed in between the people, several more gunshots rang out, and he used the seat in the first gondola to propel him to the second gondola. It shook under his weight and toppled a few people inside it. In a human game of Frogger, his foot landed on the far wooden rail of the second gondola, and he instantly pushed off again with all the bounce he had, leapt across the few feet of open water, and latched onto the top of the stone rail like a monkey on a tree branch. His feet barely had enough traction to stay on the lip of the concrete below him. As he pulled himself up and over the rail, he glanced back, and the two men chasing him pulled up short of the water he'd just leapt over. They raised their guns and spent the rest of their bullets, which clanged against the stone rail, which Xander was now ducking behind. When he heard both their guns click, their magazines empty, he rose and ran into the courtyard.

Sam came into his ear. "Xander, there are three men at the north end of the square firing on us. We are going to slip out of the square through the museum and come up behind you."

"Negative," Xander answered, his breathing labored as he ran. "I am on the port walkway now. I'll be coming up right behind the men firing on you. Hold your ground, let's take them out. Zhanna, there are two men in the street behind the museum. Take them down and we'll see where we stand. Brancati can't be far."

"On my way," Zhanna said.

"Holding here," Sam said. "But hurry."

Xander ran to the northeast entrance of the square. The iconic clock tower loomed overhead, a fingernail moon just beyond it. He sidled up to a column that held up the roof over the covered walkway and peered past the shops toward the clock tower. At its base he could see the sparks of gunfire from the men firing on Sam and Jack.

With no gun, Xander methodically crept toward them, using each column along the way as cover. He glided past the shops and restaurants along the covered path to the last column before the open space between him and the gunman at the tower. He saw two men firing into the square, then heard the bang of another gun on the other side of the tower. The three men Sam mentioned.

"We can't get out from behind the tables covering us," Sam said. "They have more ammunition than they should. They were prepared for a gunfight."

"Hold tight," Xander said. "I think I'm about to be the first man to bring a knife to one of those, and win."

5

Mission Failure

THE THREE MEN continued to fire on Sam and Jack in the middle of Piazza San Marco.

Zhanna spoke in Xander's ear. "The two men in street are down. No sign of any others."

Xander didn't respond. He was busy making a move for the two men firing on his friends. He waited until the gunman closest to him stopped to insert a fresh magazine. He arrived behind him just as the man clicked it in place. With his right hand, Xander slid his knife across the man's throat from behind, while taking the man's gun with his left. Before the second gunman even knew to react, Xander pulled back the slide on the pistol and put two bullets in his back. The gunshots from the third gunman on the other side of the tower stopped. Xander rounded the corner of the tower and shots began coming his way from the square.

"It's me! It's me!" Xander shouted as he hit the ground.

"A heads-up would have been nice," Sam said into his ear.

"What part of the whole knife-gunfight-dad joke didn't you understand?"

"The third gunman just rounded the clock tower behind you. We're moving forward."

Xander rose to his feet. The dim yellow lights in the square revealed Sam and Jack jogging toward him. A comical sight in spite of the violent circumstances. It wasn't often you got to watch a beautiful ex-MI6 agent running alongside a real-life American cowboy. Team Reign was nothing if not diverse.

"You think this third gunman could be Brancati?" Xander whispered to Sam and Jack. The three of them took cover beside the red brick wall of the clock tower.

"No," Jack and Sam said in unison.

Sam elaborated in a whisper. "I think Brancati let himself be seen by us for show. Used himself as a distraction."

"So you think he's gone?"

"I do."

Xander nodded.

"Fermo! Polizia!" a man shouted behind them. Then there were gunshots. Xander, Sam, and Jack rounded the clock tower on the opposite side of the shots fired. They could see that the police had shot and killed the third gunman. The three of them ran for the west end of the square and disappeared into the narrow streets of Venice. They hurried for the small apartment that the CIA had rented for them under a fake name, and waited for Zhanna to meet them there.

XANDER PACED the floor of the apartment, walking in circles around the coffee table in the centuries-old kitchen.

"Sam, how did we not know Sarah was going to be here in Venice tonight?" The question had been burning in Xander's mind since the moment he had locked eyes with Sarah in the museum. It had been such a shock that it almost got him killed. Director Hartsfield leaving out that little nugget of information was unacceptable.

"I'm not sure," Sam said. "I'm assuming she's in deep cover. The only information I received when I requested her to join Team Reign was that she had already been assigned."

"What is the point of having the CIA work with us if they are just going to make our lives harder?"

"None, but that's where we are. I'll find out what I can, but I doubt there will be any information for us. She's clearly in a top secret situation, or Director Hartsfield would have clued us in."

A knock at the door. Jack rounded the corner and opened the door. Zhanna stood in the doorway, alone, a red look of anger on her face that matched her fiery hair. She stalked into the apartment without saying a word. Xander exaggerated a look toward the door behind her.

"I'm assuming the police are on their way with Red Dress?"

Zhanna's angered expression didn't change. She shook her head.

"So they're holding her at the station."

It wasn't a question.

Again, Zhanna shook her head.

Xander turned, whipped his glass of bourbon across the room, the glass shattering against the far wall. The others in the room remained silent, allowing his blood to move from boil to simmer.

Xander took a calming breath and turned to his team. "Let me get this straight. We come to Venice for maybe the easiest mission I've ever been assigned: retrieve a flash drive containing sensitive information. We fail." He waits until he gets a nod from everyone. "We fail because as I am tracking the target, we find out that I am actually the target, that I'm being hunted by a world-renowned assassin." Everyone nods. "And before I can make my move, a seemingly harmless woman in a red dress tries to kill me as, oh by the way, I'm distracted by seeing one of our very own that we had no clue was even in the country, much less at the same event our target is attending. Adding insult to injury, everyone gets away, we have no idea where the flash drive is, where Sarah Gilbright is, or our target's current location, or why he or his employer wants me dead. That about sum it up?"

Xander searched everyone's eyes as they each gave a final nod.

"Awesome." The sarcasm was heavy. "I really have a good feeling about all of this. We're really on top of our game."

Sam rose from her seat. "Now that your trip down memory lane is over, Xander, let's focus on what is next."

"No thanks. I'll leave that up to you. I need to get some air."

Jack said, "I don't think that's such a good idea, son."

"Thanks, Jack. I'll take that into consideration as I walk out the door."

"You have an assassin after you and we know he is here in Venice," Sam said. "Don't be stupid."

Xander walked over to the end table beside the sofa, picked up Jack's black cowboy hat, and slid it down over his head as he looked at Jack. "You mind?"

Jack shook his head.

Xander turned to Sam. "Happy?"

Sam wasn't impressed. "Just get the hell out of here so we can get some work done."

Xander obliged and walked out the door. He was met with the damp and musty smell of the canals. He was in a particularly bad mood, and as Sarah's face flashed before his eyes, it wasn't hard to figure out why.

6

—————

To Spy or Not to Spy

As XANDER STROLLED alongside the streets of water, contemplating Sarah Gilbright and what could possibly be her involvement in his team's monumental failure in Venice, Sarah herself was contemplating Xander. The water of the lagoon lapped against the yacht's bow below her as she lapped up another martini to help calm her nerves. She managed to slip away from Andonios Maragos and his hungry hands for a quiet moment, and the only thing she could think of was how in the hell Xander King ended up at that museum. The CIA was crossing wires, and that never ended well. It put her in real danger, but she could tell by the look on Xander's face that he was just as shocked to find her there.

Not good.

A fingernail moon hung above her by an invisible string, kept company by millions of floating yellow stars. Andonios's yacht was anchored in the lagoon, making it impossible for her to make a move. Not that she would anyway. For the first time in six months, there was progress in this assignment, and she couldn't afford to make any sudden moves now. She was close.

As the cool Venetian breeze blew her long blond hair back over her shoulder, as she had often done over the past several months, she thought about how Xander and Andonios actually had a lot in common. The assignment matched Sarah well because of it. Andonios was rich, handsome, and painfully charismatic. All characteristics of her former lover Xander. The similarities ended there, however. Xander was all of those things, along with being the most highly skilled soldier and assassin that Sarah had ever seen. It didn't take long to realize this as she fought alongside him in Moscow. It only drew her to him more. Andonios, on the other hand, knew about as much about a combat situation as he knew about Sarah being in the CIA. Nothing.

When she first had her "accidental" meeting with Andonios —"the modern-day Greek god," as the press called him—he showed no signs of being anything other than a wealthy business man, traveling the world, the face of a multibillion-dollar empire. Then she met his brother. Sure, he was cordial enough at first, but there was something off about him. Sarah could tell that Gregor Maragos was not happy about his brother spending time with an American. It very well could have been a case of brotherly jealousy, but the coldness Sarah felt when Gregor was near ticked her radar to something more. The entire reason she was missioned to get close to Andonios was to find out more about Gregor's dealings. Maybe Gregor could smell that on her. Either way, she could tell something was off, but there hadn't been a lot to go on.

That is, until tonight when she was introduced to Lorenzo Russo, aka Alessio Brancati, just over an hour ago. The second he walked up to Andonios at the museum, Sarah recognized the infamous assassin. Everyone in the intelligence community knew that face. And the double gut punch of seeing Xander a few moments later was enough to knock her off her game entirely. She was fairly certain Brancati handed Andonios something in their handshake. If she didn't know anything else, she figured that was as good a place as any to start. It was time to stop being the world traveling banking consultant that was her CIA cover, and start being the special agent she was groomed to be.

Sarah finished the last of her extra dirty martini. "Extra dirty is right," Xander would have said with a wink. She then made her way through the main salon, down the stairs, and across the long hall to the closed door of the master suite where she hoped Andonios was fast asleep. She had been invited to share this room with him many times, but she had yet to accept. "Friends" was their official title. But Andonios, even though he never stopped sleeping with a myriad of other women, was growing tired of Sarah not allowing a relationship to blossom. Frankly, she was astonished herself that she had resisted him as long as she had. And even more baffled as to why he continued to pursue spending time with her even though she had never let it become romantic. She supposed she had balanced her resistance with teasing just enough to keep him hopeful. The kiss they shared a month back was enough to keep him from losing interest entirely. And she could tell by the way he looked at her on the sun deck that her bikini show hadn't hurt either. But now she needed answers. And she was going to have to get them one way or another. Sarah was prepared for whatever that required.

She tried the door handle: unlocked. Before she pushed the door inward into Andonios's room, the scenarios began to spin in her head. If he's asleep, she would search his clothing for whatever the hell was passed to him by Brancati. *If* his clothes were out in the open. If they weren't, she would do a quick search of the room, looking for something small enough to be concealed inside a man's hand. As she stood holding down the door handle in the complete silence of the hallway, ready to push inward, it occurred to her that while her CIA handler, Thomas Rodgers, wouldn't know why Xander was in Venice, he might be able to put her in touch with Director Hartsfield, who certainly would. Protocol was that no one even knew about Xander and Team Reign, but of course Sarah, having fought alongside them on more than one occasion, was the exception. Director Hartsfield knew this and could have enlightened Sarah before she went in half-cocked, not even knowing what she was looking for.

Sarah slowly eased her hand off the door handle, feeling good about not taking the chance of walking into a bad situation.

"Can I help you?"

Sarah nearly jumped out of her skin as she whirled around to face Andonios. So much for working the CIA channels.

"Andonios, you startled me." She rested a hand on his arm. "I wanted to thank you for this evening before you got to sleep, but I decided it best not to wake you."

"You know I would never mind you coming into my bedroom. Asleep or not." His brown eyes softly pleaded. Her blue eyes did their best not to lead him on.

"Crazy about the shootings in the square," she said, changing the subject. "Thank you for getting me out of there safely. I hope no one was hurt."

"Of course. And yes, crazy. I haven't heard the details."

As he spoke, Sarah decided it best to let him go on to bed. She wasn't going to be able to find what she was looking for tonight. But she would have to find out what Xander knows. And if what Xander was looking for was in fact passed from Brancati to Andonios, she was going to have to retrieve it before they left for Greece in the morning. If what Xander was looking for makes it off this boat, they would most likely have no chance of getting their hands on it again.

"Well," Sarah said as she squeezed his arm, "thank you."

Andonios nodded. "Are you sure I can't interest you in making a good night even better?"

Sarah couldn't help herself, and her eyes fell to the opening in his loosely buttoned white dress shirt. Andonios's olive skin, streaked with his dark hair flowing across his well-defined chest, made her want to say yes. But she couldn't. She needed to get some information now.

"Listen," she told him. "It's just that I've been hurt before, and—"

"I would never hurt you, Sarah."

She believed him.

Her smile faltered.

"I've had a little too much to drink. I have to be in Zurich Monday, but tomorrow night before I leave Greece, take me on a proper date?"

Andonios's eyes lit up, then quickly he played it cool. "I know of a wonderful place by the sea."

Sarah moved forward and placed a soft kiss on Andonios's lips. She immediately thought of Xander. She had expected a spark, but all that was on her mind was what exactly this man and his brother were hiding. Her libido faded as she was certain his grew. There was no way she could lay with a man who might be on the wrong side of the law. Not even for her country. She'd rather kill him first.

7

Full Moon

SITTING UP IN BED, Xander swirled the bourbon in his tumbler as he read the confidential update sent to the team on his iPad. It was going on three in the morning. Sleep would escape him tonight. Xander didn't like to lose, and tonight was a complete failure. He also couldn't help but hear Sam working the phone in the room next to him. The walls inside the ancient building were impossibly thin. Director Hartsfield sent the team the message a little over an hour ago that she had cleared all of them with the police. And the main reason there wouldn't be any sleep was because Brancati had been captured on camera leaving Venice via motorboat.

A free man.

Xander took a sip from his glass as he wondered if Sarah too had already gone. Though he knew she was more than capable, he couldn't help but worry about her. It's who he was. Also being who he was, he wanted to know who in the hell she was with, and why the man was shaking hands with an assassin. An assassin who apparently was after Xander himself.

Xander finished the bourbon in his glass, grabbed the bottle from the nightstand, and refilled. He was doing his best to flick through his mental Rolodex of bad guys who could have possibly hired Brancati. Of those who might want him dead. This wasn't the first time Xander had been in this position, but it was the first time someone of Brancati's pedigree had been the hunter. Since he left the military, Xander and Sam had gone against many a powerful man. Too many to count, and too many to try to figure out which one of the still living could be after him.

He closed his iPad and padded across the cold tile over to the window. It was a view of another window. The CIA had really gone all out on this apartment.

The door opened behind him. "Xander, I've just got off the phone with––good God, put some pants on, would you?"

Xander didn't turn to see Sam hiding her eyes. Instead, he stood like a statue, all six-foot-three and 215 pounds of him, completely naked, as if she'd never entered the room. "Full moon after all tonight."

What was the point of working to keep his body looking like a machine if he didn't show it off once in a while?

He looked over his shoulder, a boyish grin on his face, his bare ass burning in Sam's eyes.

Sam peeked through an opening in her fingers, then recovered her eyes. "Please, just once, act your age?"

"You're the one who came into my room without knocking."

Sam moved toward the bed, grabbed the top sheet, and wrapped it around Xander's waist, fixing it with a knot. "A failed mission, being hunted by an assassin, and still a smart-ass. If nothing else, Xander, you're consistent."

Xander turned toward her. "Life's short, learn to enjoy the little things."

Sam's eyes dropped toward his covered groin. "Don't suppose you mean that little thing?"

Xander smirked. "See, I knew you had it in you."

There were too many sexual puns for Xander to grab just one. So he spared Sam her usual eye roll and continued. "Heard you on the phone. You make any progress?"

"No, but Sarah has."

Xander felt something that he couldn't quite place when he heard Sarah's name. "She made contact?"

"About an hour ago. The man you saw her with was Andonios Maragos."

Xander slipped a T-shirt over his head, then removed the sheet to put on a pair of joggers. He tried to get it off before Sam could manage to turn away, but she was too quick. "Where do I know that name?"

"One of your billionaire buddies." A smirk.

A frown. "More specific?"

"Son of shipping and banking tycoon Leo Maragos."

Xander nodded. He had heard that name a few times over the years.

Sam continued. "Since Leo died, Andonios took the reins. Seems more just the face of the company than actually running anything."

"So what's the reason for Sarah being assigned to him if he's just the face of a legit company?"

"His brother." Sam showed Xander a picture on her phone. "Gregor. Nothing major on him. He was flagged for buying an abundance of listed materials many months ago, but nothing since. All could be legit as well, but they sent Sarah in to cut her teeth on an easy recon assignment."

"Cut her teeth? They didn't consider her twice saving our asses cutting her teeth?"

"Rules, Xander. This is her first undercover. And apparently the CIA made the right call deciding to send her in. We know something is going on for certain now that Andonios has made contact with Brancati. Their little hide-in-plain-sight meetup backfired."

"So it's Andonios who should be watched, not his brother?"

"Seems that way for now," Sam said. "But they are brothers, so I'm sure what one is doing, the other likely knows about."

Xander nodded. Thinking. "Where is Sarah now?"

"Anchored in the lagoon. On Andonios's yacht."

"What are we waiting for? Let's get out there." Xander made a move for his shoes.

"Put your shoes down," Sam said like a mother scolding her toddler for picking up something he wasn't supposed to. "We can't go out there. We can't risk blowing Sarah's cover."

"But the flash drive is on that boat. You know, the entire reason we are here. National security?"

"*Maybe* the flash drive is on that boat, Xander. You didn't actually see Brancati hand it to him."

"He handed it to him." He said it more confidently than he actually felt about it. Fact is, Sam was right. He didn't actually see anything. Who knows what Brancati's true intentions were in that museum.

Sam walked over to the door. "We have to trust Sarah and be patient. I know neither is your strong suit, but make an exception tonight and get some sleep."

"I don't like any of this, Sam."

"Of course you don't. You have no way of controlling it."

8

Dbie's Littles

DBIE JOHNSON OPENED the navigation app on her laptop for the 450th time of the day. Her feet hurt, her back ached, but none of that mattered. With the money they were paying her to ensure all these little machines worked, she'd stay at it until she passed out.

She pushed the laptop away for a moment. She arched her back, angling for a good stretch to get some relief. She eyed the time on her laptop: 3:32 a.m. She turned to find that she was the only one left in the building. All the other stations were empty. She had been so consumed with her work that she hadn't noticed anyone leave. She removed the earbuds from her ears so Journey could no longer tell her, "Don't Stop Believin'."

A yawn.

Another stretch.

Dbie rubbed her eyes, cracked her neck, and took a moment to try to think of nothing. Instead, all she could think of was what she had been thinking about nonstop for the last couple weeks.

"How the hell did I end up here?" She directed her question at the mechanical arms, the piles of materials, and the rest of the empty warehouse.

Not only how the hell did she end up there, but building nanobots? She felt like she'd fallen asleep and been dreaming of the future.

She reached over to her forearm and pinched herself. Not a dream. She really was stuffed in the back of some old shipping warehouse, in some remote location in Athens, Greece, with a bunch of people smarter than herself, none of whom she knew, building computer-controlled mosquitos for God knows who and for God knows what. She wasn't sure that reaching out to her government had been the right thing to do. Apparently they didn't think anything sinister was going on, because she hadn't heard a thing in days from the government official she was finally allowed to speak with on the phone. The same one who had promised to get back to her "ASAP."

Right.

Dbie's gut had told her that what she was doing was wrong. She knew it from the moment she got the email and from every strange thing they did to make sure she told no one about what she was doing for them. If she didn't need the money for all the student loans––MIT wasn't cheap––and for all of her mother's medical bills––cancer, also not cheap––she would have left weeks ago. She *should* have left weeks ago. Because now there was no doubt something terrible was happening, and here she was stuck right smack in the middle of it. Watching that sorry excuse for a man put that bullet in the back of Dr. Birschbach's head was the most frightening moment of her life. And now, knowing nothing about where she was or how to get away, her life and the lives of a whole lot of other people were squarely in danger.

This was her last quality check of the night. No sense prolonging it any longer. Dr. Emilia Kruger, now in charge after the *murder* (she still couldn't believe it actually happened), had only asked that Dbie get through 350 bots. But one thing was for certain: if Dbie had no way out of there, and apparently no support from her own government—the almighty US of A—she for damn sure was going to stay on the good side of these freaks. They ask for 350 bots, she would give them 450. They ask her to do a hundred push-ups, she'd make it two hundred (though she could never do that many). Somehow, some way, if she kept her eyes open, she knew she would find a way out of there.

Dbie pulled her laptop close, replaced her earbuds, and now Stephen Tyler and Aerosmith were telling her to "Walk This Way." All she really wanted to do was walk whatever way got her the hell out of this mess and back to her mother, who needed her now more than ever. But this was the only way they could afford the chemo she needed. So this was what she was going to do, at least until they paid her enough to take care of all the bills.

She pulled up the controls, typed in her code to power up the bot, then glanced beyond her laptop's screen to watch the red trio of lights on the back of the tiny bot light up. When the lights faded, the all-grey metal mosquito, less than a quarter of an inch in size, stared back at her, a faint glow of red in its insidious little eyes. Though hundreds of these had already passed her inspection, she still couldn't believe their capabilities. She pressed another series of buttons, and its four ultratiny wings came to life, fluttering like *Honey, I Shrunk the* Hummingbirds. She picked up the controller beside her laptop, basically a modified video game controller, and pressed the joystick upward. The faintest sound of a buzz would have been heard if Stephen Tyler wasn't still serenading her, and just as it was made to do, the minuscule little insect bot rose steadily off its platform. Floating there as if waiting for its next meal. The mosquito bot's proboscis —the straw-like antenna jutting from its head—was preloaded with dye to ensure proper functioning.

As she had done 449 times already that day, Dbie maneuvered the nanoweapon up, down, left, right, all systems working perfectly. Now that all the manual controls were functioning properly, it was time for the real test. The thing that really made this little weapon scary as hell.

Dbie put the controller down and went back to her laptop. The mosquito hovered in place as she pulled up its systems. She clicked on the camera function, and because the mosquito bot was facing her, her face materialized on the screen. The nanocamera between the nanobot's eyes watched closely as she picked up the controls again. Across the warehouse, over a hundred yards away, there was a clear gel ball sitting on a table. Using only the mosquito bot's camera, she moved the bot in the direction of the ball.

She looked up from the screen for a moment to observe the bot. It was like watching a real-life mosquito glide toward its prey. It was an absolute marvel that something so small could be controlled with such ease. Eyes back on the computer, she easily navigated the mosquito through the warehouse. Halfway there, she stopped.

"All right, now for the really scary shit," she said aloud.

Encased in the clear gel ball was a cell phone. Dbie picked up another cell phone that Dr. Kruger had given her to test the bots and went to the messages app. She texted the number code of the bot she was testing to the cell phone in the gel ball, and without touching any of the controls, Dbie watched as once again the mosquito began to move forward. This time all on its own.

Dbie picked up the laptop and began walking the path of the mosquito bot, moving toward the gel ball. When the cell phone in the ball received the text, it automatically pinged back to the mosquito bot, letting the bot know the phone's geolocation, telling it exactly where it was supposed to land. And as long as the phone maintained power and some sort of wireless connection, whether through Wi-Fi or cellular service, the mosquito bot would be able to find it.

"So scary."

Dbie watched on her screen as the mosquito landed on the gel ball and did what she had previously programmed it to do. The mosquito bot lowered its proboscis into the gel of the ball, but instead of sucking like a real mosquito would do to draw blood, it injected the dye into its silicon victim. Dbie set the laptop on a nearby table and walked over to the gel ball. Sure enough, the red dye it had been loaded with had been injected into the gel of the ball.

"Nothing good can come of this."

When they had first brought her in to work on the bots, the story they told her to explain why they were doing all of this was they hoped to be able to deliver mass amounts of medicine and vaccines to people in remote or diseased areas. She thought it sounded silly at the time, but again, the money was good. After watching Dr. Birschbach be executed in front of her, she knew her instincts were correct. The ease with which someone could be poisoned, or a deadly disease administered, by one of these bots terrified Dbie. All someone would need was the ability to control the bot manually, to make it land on someone, either by entering their GPS coordinates or simply knowing their cell phone number. A weapon of this magnitude had never been seen by humanity. Now there was no need for things like nuclear weapons. Presidents, dictators, prime ministers, and even kings could be surgically removed from power with the use of a cell phone, whether a mile or three thousand miles away. Or an entire city's water supply could be tainted. And all the sinister ways these bots could ruin humanity could go on and on.

With this new invisible nanotechnology, no one was safe. Not even the most well-guarded leaders in the world. And in that moment the thing that scared Dbie the most wasn't that she might not make it out of there alive. It was the fact that no matter where someone was in the world, if Gregor Maragos deemed that someone unworthy, they wouldn't make it out alive either.

9

In a Flash

"Do you have it?" Gregor wasted no time getting to the point with his brother. He'd waited all night to talk to him. This was the fifth time he had called since six in the morning.

"What the hell is going on, Gregor?" There was fear in Andonios's voice. "Whatever you had me do last night almost got me killed. I want no part of this. Do you understand me?"

"I said, do you have it?" Gregor's tone held a little more ice.

"What I have is a madman for a brother. How did you end up like this? Not enough attention from Daddy? I mean, what do you do all day in father's old shipping warehouse? What are you working on that is so secretive, and that has people getting into shoot-outs in Venice over it? Whatever you are doing, it's time to stop."

Gregor took a deep breath. Finesse was not his strong suit, but he felt he had to give it his best shot if he was going to keep his brother, the poor fool, from ruining all of the hard work he'd done on the nanobots.

"Andonios, tell me you have what I need and I will explain everything."

He heard Andonios let out a frustrated huff. "I have it. Now tell me why people are dying for it."

Gregor knew to play into his brother's greed. "Because, my brother, whatever fortune our father built will pale in comparison to what I have created."

Silence.

"It will bring fame and fortune, the likes of which you've never seen."

Still quiet. Then a moment later Andonios asked, "How much money are we talking about?"

The exact words Gregor was hoping to hear.

"Limitless."

Now a hint of excitement in Andonios's voice. "But . . . how?"

"Every military in the world will be outbidding each other for what I have created." Gregor had no intention of selling a thing.

"You've built a weapon?"

"No, Andonios. I've built THE weapon. The quintessence of modern warfare."

Another moment of silence. "You have a priceless weapon, and you put it on a flash drive? How could you be so careless?"

Gregor always thought Andonios to be clueless. This only further proved it. "No, Andonios. I have a mole on my team. The flash drive contains a phone conversation from that mole that could kill this entire deal before we can reap the benefits."

"I don't understand. How did this man who handed me the flash drive come to have it in his possession? Wouldn't the person who your so-called mole told about your operation still be able to leak the information on the flash drive?"

Gregor was afraid his brother would ask this question. Andonios's greed ran deep, but the line would most definitely be drawn at murder. Telling Andonios that he hired one of the world's most renowned assassins to retrieve the flash drive and eliminate the CIA agent who had recorded it would most certainly make Andonios turn sour. This was Gregor's fear when he had to involve Andonios in the first place. But there had been no choice. Gregor couldn't leave Greece and the operation at this critical juncture, and Brancati already having to be in Venice for other business was too perfect not to have Andonios retrieve the flash drive from him. And Gregor could especially not leave the operation right now, not with a mole on staff. He'd hoped killing Dr. Birschbach in front of everyone would discourage any more attempts to speak out against the project, but he had to stay in Greece until he was certain nothing else would get out. That was what today was all about: finding the mole. Since it was the CIA that had been contacted, most likely it was one of the three Americans on his team of scientists and engineers. But he couldn't afford to lose any of them at the moment. Not if he wanted this army of nanobots built in the next week. He would discover who the mole was as soon as the flash drive was in his possession.

"Gregor," Andonios prompted.

"It is none of your concern, brother. My security team is the best in the world, and they have it handled. As long as you have the right flash drive, that is. I need it here this afternoon. Don't do anything with it. Don't even listen to it. I don't want to endanger you more than I already have. Just get on the plane and bring it to me."

Gregor waited as his brother was quiet. All he could do was hope Andonios's greed outweighed his curiosity and fears.

"I'll leave within the hour."

Gregor ended the call and turned to Dr. Kruger who sat across from him in his office. "It is done. Now, bring me the three Americans."

"You're sure he can make it back here without any problems?

There was the shoot-out in Venice last night. Someone is obviously sniffing around. What if they get to Andonios before he can get out of Italy?"

Gregor smiled the smile of an alligator who'd found his prey. "I thought of this already. I have already called for backup. There will be no problems getting Andonios back here safely, flash drive in hand."

10

I'll Be Watching You

THE YELLOW-ORANGE FIREBALL of life peeked its head up from behind the blue curtain of the lagoon. Xander looked on from the water's edge. Gondolas bobbed along the top of that lagoon as the water lapped against the concrete walkway. Morning chatter from patrons sipping espresso and discussing the day's adventure filled the gap behind him. They were probably gossiping about last night's shoot-out as well. Until then, they had been blissfully unaware of the chaos that surrounded them. That always surrounded them. Just beyond their realm of understanding.

The sunrise, as always, was a beautiful sight. However, it caused a pang of longing inside Xander. He closed his eyes and put himself on the back porch of his home in Lexington, Kentucky. The beautiful bluegrass of the rolling hills waving in a summer breeze just beyond the steeple that stood proudly atop his prized Thoroughbreds' stable. He was missing home.

Over the last year he'd spent very little time there. Since all that had happened in Syria, Moscow, Paris, etcetera, and since joining forces with the CIA, he'd become disconnected from his businesses, from his old life entirely. He missed his sister and his niece, but there were only so many hours in a day. And though he loved his horses and his bourbon company, his real passion was using what the US military had trained him to do: fight.

It wasn't just the end result that made him love fighting for his country. It was the struggle of the entire journey where he thrived. That's how he knew he wasn't meant for anything else. When you find something in life worth struggling for, something you actually *love* struggling for, you know you've found something worth doing. Xander really didn't know what that said about him. Whether it was a good or a bad thing. But he was certain of one thing: a man who enjoys moments when bullets are flying toward him, when trained killers are hunting him, and when running away from the chaos feels like the *wrong* thing to do . . . well, that man at his core, though he may be many things, is a crazy son of a bitch.

Xander's phone buzzed in his pocket. Sam. He couldn't so much as find a moment to daydream about home without being interrupted.

"Brancati never left Venice."

Xander pulled his hat lower on his head and took two steps to his right, putting the black wooden beam of the gondola stand between him and Piazza San Marco behind him. They had known this was a possibility. That's why Xander had left the apartment so early, why he'd worn the hat, and why Sam, Jack, and Zhanna went ahead of him to scout a safe route to the airport. Xander had protested at first, but Sam was right: you can't be too careful when a man like Brancati is after you.

"Where are you, Sam?" Xander asked.

"Jack and I are at the top of the parking garage. I took a water route here, Zhanna and Jack took two separate walking routes. Zhanna is on a bench by the water."

"And?"

"No one can be certain, but I believe my route is the safest. Rent a water taxi, stay down inside the covered cabin until you reach the drop point just below me."

"Get Zhanna out of there," Xander said. "No sense throwing up any red flags. She may not look like a CIA agent, but we don't know what Brancati knows about our team."

"Good idea. I'm turning on our COM system, but continue to talk like you are on the phone."

Sam ended the call, then he heard her come back inside his ear. "When you put away the phone, no more talking."

"If Brancati is watching me that close, I'm already a dead man."

"Then get your ass in a water taxi and let's get the hell out of here. You are a sitting duck out in the open. I can come back to you."

"There's no time."

"Agreed," Sam said. "Jack has his eye on you. We'll be able to let you know if any suspicious boats approach your water taxi in the lagoon."

Xander pictured the old man peering through the scope of his Barrett .50 caliber sniper rifle. He couldn't help but feel a little bit safer. But not safe enough. He needed to get going. Twenty-five feet to his right there was a water taxi dock. He waited for a group of people to walk by and then fell in step with them, crouching as much as possible without looking out of place.

"Okay, my life is in your hands," Xander said. He put the phone in his pocket.

"Make this quick," he heard Sam in his ear. "The longer we are here, the worse our odds of leaving."

Xander stayed with the group of foreigners until he arrived at the water taxi stand. There was a woman ahead of him standing at the entrance to the dock waiting for a taxi. Sam said something in his ear, but whatever it was never made it from Xander's ear to his brain. He was too busy staring at the left hand of the dark-haired woman in front of him.

Staring at the black heart tattoo at the base of her thumb.

The moment it registered that it was the woman in the red dress, something poked him in the back, and a hand wrapped swiftly and tightly around his right arm.

A man spoke firmly. "No sudden moves. Start walking, and don't even think about turning around." Whoever this man was, it was clear he was changing his voice to disguise it.

Xander did as he was told. A gun pointed at your back is always a fairly good reason to comply. Just as they started walking away, he sensed Red Dress watching him, but he couldn't discern what move she made. She didn't come at him, so whoever had the gun in his back must be working with her. Must be working for Brancati. Brancati must want Xander alive. Not good.

"Xander, who is that?" He heard Sam in his ear. "Do not go wherever he is taking you. On the count of three, drop to the ground, Jack will put him down."

The man said, "Tell Jack to put the sniper rifle away."

A chill ran down Xander's spine.

"One." Sam began her count.

Xander knew Brancati was good, but if he knew all the way down to Jack watching him with a sniper rifle, they were all dead.

"Two."

"Tell him!" the man shouted, still disguising his voice with a low grumble.

"Thre—!"

"Jack, don't shoot!"

For a moment, all of Venice seemed quiet. Maybe because all Xander could hear through his pounding heartbeat was the rush of blood pulsing in his ears. The breeze continued to blow. First he heard the coo of the seagulls, then a horn from somewhere in the lagoon, then the crowd noise finally returning to his ears. As did the gun in his back as the man yanked him to the right, into an alley.

"Xander!" Sam shouted. "Don't let him take you to into that alley!"

Xander's wits returned. He slid his left hand into his pocket and wrapped his fingers around his knife.

"Take your hands off the knife," the man said as he pushed Xander a couple feet away from him. "And reach your hands for the sky."

The man knew everything about Xander. And everything about where his team was situated. Something wasn't right. Something was—

The man's voice changed. No longer disguised. And he was singing. "Now put your right leg in and you shake it all about."

"The Hokey Pokey"?

Kyle.

Xander turned to find his oldest friend in the world, and apparently the newest confirmed member of the CIA, Kyle Hamilton. Xander knew his smile was as wide as Kyle's. He couldn't be happier to see his partner in crime. "I can't believe they actually passed you." Xander moved in and gave Kyle a hug. His six-foot-three-inch frame had become even more chiseled since the last time Xander had seen him. The CIA must have really put him through the paces. Xander backed away to get a good look at him.

"Highest score in ten years, brother." Kyle's smile turned into a confident smirk.

"What are you saying? Who is that? Xander, are you all right?" Sam didn't panic often, but there was deep concern in her voice. And as her voice had done countless times over the years, intentionally or not, it brought Xander focus.

Red Dress.

"What?" Kyle asked, obviously seeing a shift in Xander's demeanor.

Xander grabbed Kyle by his jacket lapels and pulled him down to the ground behind the dumpster. Gunshots rang out from the entrance to the alleyway, just missing the two of them.

"Jack, purple jacket, dark hair. Take her down."

"Brancati?" Kyle asked as he reached for his pistol.

Xander didn't answer. Three more shots rang out, and just as Xander took a peek from behind the dumpster, the top of Red Dress's head went missing from the rest of her body.

"We've gotta move," Xander told Kyle. "What do you know?"

Xander helped Kyle to his feet, then began to walk quickly down the alley, away from Red Dress's body.

Kyle followed. "Everything. That's why I pulled you from the waterway. Brancati's still here in Venice."

"I know, that was his girlfriend Jack just put down," he told Kyle. Then to everyone listening on his COM, Xander announced, "Red Dress is down, Kyle and I are moving inward. What's it look like by the water?"

"Kyle?" Sam came back, flabbergasted.

"Sam! What's it look like on the street?"

"A crowd around her body. No one else looks suspicious. You're clear waterside."

"You're sure?"

"Right now there is no one coming your way. Get to a motorboat and get here, now!"

Xander stopped and looked back toward the alley entrance about a hundred yards away. He saw the crowd around the dead woman. Beyond them, what looked like a small speedboat was tied off at the dock.

Sam continued, "There's a white motorboat tied off directly across from you in the lagoon. Jack can cover you. If Red Dress was coming from this end, I bet someone else will be coming from the other side."

Xander glanced back toward the opposite end of the alley. No sign of anyone. Something wasn't right. Xander and Team Reign had botched every aspect of this mission. So much so that Kyle was able to spot Xander in the crowd. If he could do that, Brancati could.

Someone was playing games.

Xander may have lost the first quarter, but Brancati was playing with fire by letting him stay in the game.

11

All Aboard

"I'LL LEAVE WITHIN THE HOUR."

Sarah heard Andonios end the call with his brother. Her patience had paid off, but her worst fears had been confirmed. Not only did Andonios have the flash drive holding a recorded phone call, but the phone call was clearly about some sort of weapon. Now it made sense to her why a fellow agent was killed. The secrets that were being kept weren't just about money; they were what the CIA had feared, they were about national security.

As Sarah backed away from the door to Andonios's room, she couldn't help but feel proud. She was new to this espionage thing, and one of the most important traits for a spy were instincts. She knew the moment she met Andonios's brother, Gregor, that something was odd about him. She could almost see the slime dripping off him. This confirmed it, and it confirmed that she needed to continue to dial in to her gut. And follow it. Right now, however, it was telling her two different things.

On one hand, it was simple. She could easily go in and take the flash drive from him. But was that the best decision for the long game? It would obviously blow her cover. What if what is on that flash drive isn't enough information for the CIA to go on? What if it doesn't name anyone or any place specifically? If she went with Andonios back to Greece, she could part ways with him at the airport, then follow him to where he was meeting up with his brother.

But what if something went sideways and she lost sight of Andonios . . . and then didn't see where they were building whatever weapon they were building? What if the flash drive specifically says all of that and more . . . like what the weapon is, and who they are planning to sell it to, or worse, who they're planning to use it on?

Sarah couldn't chance losing the information on the flash drive.

A bird in the hand . . .

Sarah turned back toward Andonios's bedroom and knocked on the door.

"One moment," Andonios said.

The door opened, and the smile on his face that usually expressed excitement to see her now looked to be a nervous façade.

"Sarah, good morning. We'll be leaving shortly. Gather your things and I'll have Gina take them to our water taxi." Andonios remained standing in front of the door.

Sarah nudged forward, a hand on his chest. "Actually, do you mind if I speak with you for just a moment?"

Andonios resisted at first but then let her push her way inside. "I really must finish packing my things, Sarah. Can't this wait for the plane ride?"

Sarah walked around the king bed, past the gaudy golden fixtures surrounded by even gaudier brown marble, and over to the window that overlooked the lagoon. "I'm afraid it can't."

Andonios shut the door.

Sarah turned toward him, her heart pounding. This was it.

"I know about the—"

A loud beep coming from the phone by the bed interrupted Sarah.

Flash drive, she wanted to finish. Instead, a man's voice came in through the intercom.

"Mr. Maragos, there is a Mister . . ." There was a pause, some muffled conversation, then the man continued, "A Mr. Ricci, Michael Ricci, here to see you."

Andonios walked over to the phone and pressed a button. "I don't know a Michael Ricci."

Sarah's gut told her this was about to get complicated. They were anchored in the middle of the lagoon. Someone would have to have come to them by boat. They wouldn't do that unless they knew they would be able to speak with Andonios. And since Andonios clearly wasn't expecting someone, this wasn't good.

The man spoke through the intercom system again. "Says your brother sent him and to check your phone."

Andonios walked to the end of the bed and picked up his cell phone. Sarah leaned back against the dresser so she could feel the security of her Glock 17 tucked at the back of her waistline. She watched as Andonios read something on the screen. His face gave away nothing. He put away his phone and once again pressed the intercom button.

"Let him aboard. Tell him I'll meet him in the salon."

"Roger."

"Sarah, I'm afraid this conversation *will* have to wait."

"Is everything all right?"

"Perfectly fine." He stuffed a few items into a duffel bag. "Are your things ready? We must get going now."

Sarah nodded. "I'll get my bag."

Andonios turned his back to her and opened the door. She

reached behind her back and pulled her gun, pointing it at his back.

"But before I do, I need the flash drive."

Andonios stopped just before he exited the open door. The look on his face when he turned to find Sarah holding a gun on him was like he'd been hit with a taser. He dropped his bag and instinctively held up his hands.

"What? Sarah, what are you doing? Why do you have a gun?"

"The flash drive, Andonios."

He turned and took a step forward. "Who are you?"

"That's close enough. If you take one more step without the drive in your hand, I will shoot you."

Andonios swallowed hard. If it wasn't already clear to Sarah that Andonios had zero involvement in whatever was going on, looking at him now, it was crystal.

"S-Sarah, I don't know what you're talking about."

Sarah had two options: rush him, put the gun to his head, and make him give it to her, or play to his sensibilities and tell him that she can help him get out of whatever trouble he is in before he makes a mistake that will ruin the rest of his life. The problem was the unknown. Whoever had just shown up to speak with Andonios could pose a problem. What if he was also here for the flash drive? Clearly Andonios didn't know him. But whatever he read on his phone had compelled him to let a complete stranger on his boat.

"Who is Michael Ricci?" She went with option three: gather more information.

"Sarah, what is this? You heard me tell my security that I didn't know this Mr. Ricci."

"Right, then you read a text message on your phone and let a total stranger aboard. So who is he? Let me help you, Andonios. Your brother isn't telling you everything. You are in serious trouble here. You saw what happened last night after that man handed you the flash drive. You want more people shooting at you today?"

"Says the woman pointing a gun at me."

Time for a bluff. "I know everything, Andonios. And so does my government. A CIA agent was killed two nights ago for the very flash drive you now possess. You think this is going to just go away?"

"Killed?" Andonios stood up straight, another look of shock. "He didn't say anything about anyone dying."

All the information was here. She'd heard enough listening in on his phone call with Gregor, and now he just accidentally admitted to his brother's guilt. It was time to get this flash drive, and get Andonios to safety. And even more important, get word to Xander that Gregor Maragos was behind everything.

"Everything okay in there, Andonios?"

Both Sarah and Andonios were startled by the man's voice in the doorway. Sarah's stomach did another loop entirely when she noticed the man, now holding his own gun on Andonios, was the man using Michael Ricci as yet another alias. For the second time in twelve hours she was looking into the eyes of the notorious assassin Alessio Brancati.

12

Marco...

XANDER WATCHED a jet land from the window of the private aviation area of the Venice Marco Polo Airport. He was feeling a little helpless. They were awaiting word from Director Hartsfield, who was awaiting word from Sarah. Everyone was hoping she would be able to tell them who, what, or at least where they would be going next. Xander was also trying to piece together the last twenty-four hours and why they were able to slip out of Venice without tangling with Brancati. It was almost as if running into Red Dress had been a coincidence. As if the reason she was waiting at that gondola stand wasn't to trap him. Unless Brancati saw her get taken out and decided it was best to regroup and come for Xander later. Which could be the case. If he felt he was outnumbered and his element of surprise had evaporated, Brancati would possibly look for a better time to strike.

"Marco!" Kyle shouted from the opposite end of the building.

It was good to have his friend back in the fold. Though he was now a fully trained agent, it obviously hadn't dampened his personality. Thank God.

"Polo!" Xander shouted back, but his usual enthusiasm wasn't there.

Kyle walked over to him. "That was weak. Everything okay?"

"I'm worried about Sarah."

"What else is new? She'll be fine, X. You've seen her fight. She can handle herself."

Of course he was right. Sam was probably the only woman more skilled than Sarah. And she had the guts too. That combination made for someone who could easily take care of herself.

Kyle plowed through Xander's pause. "So where we headed?"

"That's the holdup. We're not sure. How are things with you and Sam? Awkward?" Xander was referring to the recent breakup.

"Nah. She's a little salty, but that's how she always is. We ended on good terms. I don't feel awkward at all."

"Good. We don't have time for bullshit." Xander didn't mince words. "If there is anything weird between you, squash it now. I have a feeling things are about to get crazy."

"All good." Kyle gave a faltering smile. "And that's scary hearing *you* say things are going to get crazy."

"I've got a bad feeling about all of this."

Kyle laughed. "Whatever for? You only have"—he used his fingers to make air quotes—"*the world's greatest assassin* after you."

"Yeah, there's that. But it's the information on that flash drive I'm more worried about."

Kyle's face became more serious. "You think it's something that big, huh?"

"For someone to kill a CIA agent over it, and get the attention of the United States Fighting Machine? Yeah, I think it's that big."

"Damn."

Sam walked up. "Bad news. Last night after Sarah made contact with Director Hartsfield, they set up a hard check-in time this morning. She didn't check in. No call, no text . . . nothing."

Kyle said, "By just a few minutes? Can't be that bad, right? She could still check in."

"I don't like this, Sam." Xander ignored Kyle. "There is too much at stake here."

"I agree with you."

"What did Zhanna say?"

Sam and Xander had agreed earlier that Zhanna would stay behind with Jack and watch Andonios Maragos's rented yacht from afar. They were to keep their distance at all costs, allowing Sarah to do her job and maintain her cover.

"She said a water taxi pulled up several minutes ago, but no movement since. It is still waiting at the back of the yacht."

Xander was frustrated. "They are getting ready to move. What the hell are we doing? Why aren't we down there?"

Sam put a hand on her hip. "We *are* down there. Jack and Zhanna have eyes on her."

"You know what I mean, Sam."

"*We* . . ."—she made a motion that included the three of them standing there—"are here to keep you out of harm's way. I'm sure I don't need to remind you that there is a target on your back."

"You know full well that if Brancati were going to make a move, he would have done it with Red Dress. You know I'm no good at just sitting back and waiting. Especially when one of us is in danger."

"Sarah is fine, Xander. She can—"

"Handle herself," Xander said, cutting Sam off. Then he pointed back and forth between her and Kyle. "Yeah, I know. The two of you plan this little speech?"

Sam and Kyle shared a glance. Kyle said, "Pretty sure Sam

and I are done sharing things. Let's get back out there if it makes you feel better, X. I agree, standing around here is pointless."

Sam didn't like where this was headed. "Great. So happy to have the pair of you back together so you can both talk each other into doing stupid shit. Makes my life so much easier."

13

A Real Sweetheart

When Andonios didn't answer, Brancati moved his gun to Sarah. "Put the gun down, sweetheart. It's your only shot at getting off this boat alive."

Sarah's heart rate jumped a few beats, but not because he was pointing a gun at her. She hated it when men who didn't know her called her sweetheart. Her stepdad used to do it on a daily basis growing up, and he only ever meant it in the most condescending way. She held her ground and didn't respond. Brancati was a good-looking man. Dark hair, tanned skin, and that smooth Italian accent. He wasn't very big, but clearly fit. And now his face began to look annoyed.

Brancati moved the gun back to Andonios. "Look, I'm not the type to wait for the dust to settle. I don't know who you are, but I will shoot him if you don't put down your gun."

As her mom used to say, Sarah had gotten herself into a real pickle. She wasn't sure why thoughts of her past kept creeping in on her as the tension rose. Was this her mind's way of flashing her life before her eyes? If so, where were all the good parts?

"Sarah, please do as he says." There was fear in Andonios's voice. A look of panic on his face.

"Yes, sweetheart. Do as I say."

Sarah turned abruptly, squeezed the trigger, and shot Brancati. She had been overthinking everything. Now was the time for action. Andonios dropped to the floor with the sound of the loud bang in the small room, and Brancati fell back into the hallway just outside the door with a shout of pain. Sarah took advantage of the moment, lunging forward to pick up Andonios's bag from the bed, crouched for a moment of cover, and unzipped the duffel.

"You bitch! You shot me!" Brancati shouted from the hall. She must not have hit him in a critical spot.

"Don't move from that hallway, Brancati," Sarah warned him.

"You know who I am?"

"The entire law enforcement world knows who you are."

His tone shifted from anger back to his smooth, slick demeanor. "Ah, you are American agent. There are quite a few of you in the city. Must be something big going on." Brancati sounded smug. "I have a good success rate with your kind. The two agents watching this boat right now are the latest to understand how dangerous it is to follow me."

Sarah didn't take the bait. She didn't know if he was speaking about the agent killed two nights ago or about Xander, but she had to focus on finding the flash drive and getting the hell off that boat. She figured his comment about the two agents watching the boat was a bluff. She had no one with her on this mission. After a few more swipes through Andonios's bag, her hand found the flash drive. However, her relief at finding it was short-lived. Her body tensed when a familiar noise off in the distance caused her to huddle behind the bed.

"See, now things have shifted once again." Brancati sounded proud. "I know you hear that. That's our ride."

The helicopter was close. It would be landing on the helipad at the back of the yacht at any moment. Sarah was about to be outnumbered.

"I've got to hand it to you, this is the first time I have been shot in years. I underestimated you."

Sarah didn't respond. She put the flash drive in her pocket and readied her gun.

Brancati continued, "But this is what I do. Like any good poker player, I always leave myself an out."

The helicopter was right overhead now. The rotors were loud, and the boat began to rock in the water from the swirling waves produced by the wind.

"You've nowhere to go, sweetheart. You have to come through me to get out of here. And even if you managed that, I have three men in the helicopter waiting for you."

Brancati was right. She was trapped, and she knew it. There was no way out. Sarah rose, fired two rounds into the hallway with her right hand, and pulled her cell phone out of her pocket with her left. Even if she wasn't going to make it out of there alive, she had to let someone know what she knew. She had to take the power away from these people and, at the very least, render the flash drive useless. It's the only way she could help her country. Whatever happened after that would be erased from history anyway, so might as well do what she can to make a difference now.

14

Shots Fired

XANDER, Kyle, and Sam walked out to the parking lot at the airport to their rented SUV. They had been waiting in Venice for some direction on where to go next. Xander had won the argument with Sam on no longer staying put. He was ready to go help Zhanna and Jack keep an eye on Sarah. Doing something, anything, was better than just sitting on his hands.

Just as they got inside the car, Xander's phone dinged a text message alert, and Sam's phone began to ring. They shared a glance, Sam turning from the front passenger seat.

"It's Zhanna," Sam said.

"It's a message from Sarah," Xander said.

Xander's emotions were split right down the middle. The text message meant Sarah was alive, but at the same time it could be a call for help. He slid his finger over the screen and opened the message. At the same time, Sam answered Zhanna's call.

"Where do we stand?" Sam said. Sam continued to talk, but

Xander didn't hear her words. His mind was focused on Sarah's text.

Gregor Maragos is building a weapon. Brancati is here. They're going to take me.

"Xander."

Xander was trying to wrap his mind around the message.

"Xander, Sarah's in trouble."

Building a weapon. Sarah must be alluding to what is on the flash drive. But she is going to be taken by Brancati? Just as the pieces began to come together, Sam finally got his attention.

"Xander! What did Sarah's message say?"

Xander snapped out of it. "What did Zhanna say?"

"That there is a helicopter landing on Andonios's yacht. She needs to know what to do. Is Sarah safe?" Sam was holding the phone away from her ear. It was on speaker, which is why all three of them in that car could hear the gunshots. And all three shared the same look of concern.

"Zhanna!" Sam shouted. "Zhanna, are you all right?" Xander hadn't heard panic in Sam's voice like that in a long time. Her cool and stern demeanor had been rocked, and it further tightened Xander's chest. There was no answer, only more gunfire.

"Kyle, get us to them, now!" Xander shouted.

Kyle started the SUV, threw it in reverse and smoked the tires as he hurried out of the parking lot.

"Zhanna!" Sam shouted again.

Xander exited the messages app on his phone, pulled up Jack's contact, and pressed call.

"Which way?" Kyle asked.

"Right," Sam answered. "Follow this road to the roundabout and make a right. I'll direct you from there!"

As Kyle followed Sam's directions, Xander listened to Jack's phone ring for the third, then the fourth time. A cold, icy feeling curled its way up the back of Xander's spine. Sarah was in trouble, but Jack and Zhanna might have had it even worse. As the

SUV roared down the road, the three of them listened to silence from Zhanna's phone and an automatic voice message on Jack's.

"Zhanna!" Sam gave it one last try.

Silence.

"Holy shit, guys, this isn't good," Kyle said, stating the obvious. Neither Xander nor Sam responded. The SUV's engine roared as Kyle took a hard right turn. Xander ended his call to Jack's phone, and just as Sam was about to do the same with Zhanna's, they heard something on the line.

"Zhanna?" Sam called out. "Zhanna, are you there? Are you all right?"

Another sound.

"Was that a man?" Kyle said.

"Sounded like a groan. A man groaning." Xander's stomach turned. He knew what they were listening to was a disaster.

"Jack?" Sam shouted. "Jack, is that you?"

They heard another sound. It was loud enough this time to understand that Xander was right. It *was* a man groaning.

Then the line went dead.

15

Dead to Rights

IT HAD ONLY BEEN a couple hours since she knocked off for the night, but Dbie was already back at it. As she stared into the little red eyes of yet another nanobot, the sound of Dr. Kruger's monotone voice right behind her was almost enough to make her jump out of her seat.

"You will follow me."

Dbie's stomach dropped. She turned to find a scowl fixed to Dr. Kruger's face. The smoker's wrinkles around her pursed lips frowned, her dark hair bobbed just below her ears, and her furrowed brow narrowed her eyes into a menacing stare. The first thing that popped into Dbie's mind when she took in Kruger's glare was the phone calls she'd made trying to contact the US government. The second thing that popped into her head was her old boss's brains flying out of his forehead after the bullet from Gregor's gun shot through his skull.

Dbie swallowed hard. "Is everything all right?"

"It will be."

That's all she said. *It will be.* Two men stepped around Kruger, and each grabbed one of Dbie's arms, pulling her up from her chair.

Dbie whipped her arms from the grasp of the men. "All right, I'm going." She didn't like men touching her. It triggered something that had long lain dormant. They reached for her again, but she maneuvered away. "I said I'm going."

"Will there be a problem, Ms. Johnson?"

"What's this about? Is there something wrong with my work?"

Kruger smiled. "Quite the opposite. But Mr. Maragos would like a word."

The only thing Dbie heard was "but." This wasn't good. What was she thinking contacting anyone about the work she was doing there? Of course these people would find out. Why couldn't she just keep her head down and do her job. All she had to do was last another week without saying a word. Now her mother would suffer, all because Dbie "Do-gooder" Johnson couldn't shut the hell up and just make a bunch of money. But Dbie knew it wouldn't have been just another week. Once Maragos met his quota for nanobots, he would just want more. And they would find a way to keep her here until God knows when.

Kruger motioned for Dbie to follow. As a million terrible thoughts floated through Dbie's mind, she couldn't help but notice Kruger walked like she had a foot-long stick up her ass. The two men moved in behind Dbie, supposedly to keep her from making a run for it. If she ran, they would find her. If Maragos knows she tried to contact the FBI and the CIA, she was in trouble.

Another thought crossed her mind. She was the only person in the entire operation who could make these little weapons mobile. After Gregor shot the doctor (the only other person who could do what she does) in the head, she was supposed to train another person as a backup, but when the timeline got moved up and Maragos wanted more bots, there was no time. This could be the very thing that saves her. For now.

Kruger walked her into Maragos's office. His back was turned to the door as he looked out the window over the empty green space behind the remote warehouse.

"Leave us," Maragos said without turning around.

Kruger and the goon squad did as Maragos asked.

"You know what I love about technology?" Maragos still gazed out the window.

Was this guy serious? Dbie remembered hearing somewhere that whenever you're in a meeting for the first time, you should find something in the office to connect with. That will help you ease into a comfortable conversation. A quick glance around the room gave her nothing. White walls, brown IKEA office furniture, and a computer. That's it. This guy was Mr. I Don't Connect.

Dbie quipped, "You can watch reruns of *Big Bang Theory* on your cell phone?" Idiot. A nervous tick was to say something funny, but it always came out sounding more smart-ass.

Gregor turned to her from the window. He was a cross between Dilbert and Rick Moranis from *Honey, I Shrunk the Kids.* Except there was something evil inside him. Dbie could just sense it. Maybe it was his lizard smile, or it could have been the fact that she watched him blow a man's head off a day ago.

"No, I've no time for simpleminded things like television. What I love about technology is that, unlike humans, it never lies."

Dbie could actually hear the gulp when she swallowed. He knew.

"Do you have anything you would like to tell me, Ms. Johnson?"

"Dbie. You can call me Dbie."

Yeah, 'cause that's what he wanted to hear.

Gregor didn't call her Dbie. He instead waited for an answer. The only thing she could think of was to make herself sound invaluable.

"I am a hundred bots ahead of schedule."

One side of Gregor's mouth moved upward. Maybe it was a smile.

"I am aware of this. Unfortunately, it isn't your work that I wanted to speak with you about."

He waited.

So did Dbie.

"It is what you have been doing with your time off."

She knew it hadn't, but it felt to her like the air in the room had thickened. Her stomach was in knots. She imagined this is what her mother feels like every time she goes in for chemo. A sickening sense of impending doom. If her mother could face death, so could she.

"Dr. Kruger said it was okay to raid the lounge refrigerator."

If the uptick on one side of Gregor's face had been a smile a moment ago, it had just dropped to a frown.

"Is this a game to you, Ms. Johnson?"

Dbie shook her head. For once, she kept her mouth shut.

"Because it isn't to me."

Silence held for a moment as they looked at each other. Dbie just wished he'd get it over with already. Whatever this meeting was.

Gregor moved toward his desk and picked up a cell phone. He tapped a couple times on the screen, then looked back at her. "What is it you think we are doing here, Ms. Johnson?"

More questions. This guy really loved to hear himself talk.

"I don't really care, to be honest with you. I'm just here for the benefits." Dbie tried to smile, though she knew that was too far. Her mother was right: her mouth was going to get her killed one day. Looks like that day had come.

Gregor didn't laugh. "You know, it's a shame you are a traitor. I think you and I would have really gotten along well."

Dbie didn't have a one-liner for that. The word traitor rang in her head like a church bell. "Traitor? Look, Mr. Maragos, I'm just doing my job."

Gregor pressed something on his phone, then held the phone to his ear. After a moment, he began to shake his head.

"Shall I play this for you?" he asked her. "Or would you like to just go ahead and tell me what you said?"

Dbie actually began to shake in her seat. "I-I don't know what you mean."

"Fine." Gregor pulled the phone away from his ear. "My security just messaged me something very concerning." He tapped again on his phone.

Dbie almost passed out. The next thing she heard was her own voice, the words she had spoken to the government official who was supposed to be helping her get out of there. She listened, fear holding her hostage.

"I'm telling you, something is going on here. They are saying these bots are to be used to deliver medicine to remote places and other bullshit. But we are building lethal and undetectable weapons here."

Gregor clicked something on his phone again. "I suppose you are going to tell me that wasn't you speaking to someone from America about what you think is going on here?"

Dead to rights.

Gregor continued, "Nothing to say now after so much to say before?"

Dbie just hung her head.

"I didn't think so." He rounded the desk and sat on its edge facing her. "Remember the next thing that was said? When the person you were lying to about my operation told you they were going to get back to you ASAP?"

Dbie looked up at Gregor. She'd never been so scared in all her life. She nodded.

"And they haven't gotten back to you, have they, Ms. Johnson?"

Dbie shook her head. Tears hung on for dear life inside her bottom eyelids.

"That's because they are dead."

The tears fell when she gave a shocked blink hearing Gregor's words. She began to shake her head. "No, that's not true."

"They are dead because of the lies you told them. They are dead because of you."

The room began to spin. What had she done? What was going to happen to her now?

Gregor's voice was cold. "I need a reason you shouldn't share a similar fate."

Her mind was jumping in a million directions, but they all scattered and one image shined through. Her mother. She had to stay alive for her mother. Slowly, focus began to return. She knew now wasn't the time to play dumb. She had to play the only card she had left and hope it would be enough to keep her alive. She cleared her throat, and with all the confidence she could muster, she looked that nerdy bastard dead in his black beady eyes . . .

"I'm the only one who knows how to get these bots ready for deployment."

16

Man Down

THE PARKING GARAGE that overlooked the lagoon in Venice was already buzzing like a beehive. By the time they made it there from the airport to see what happened to Jack and Zhanna, there were polizia everywhere, and they worked fast. An ambulance roared past them from the entrance to the parking garage that was blocked off. Kyle looked from the ambulance to Xander, worry in his eyes. It took a few heated phone calls back and forth between CIA headquarter point man for Team Reign, Marvin Cameron, and the Venice police department before they finally let Xander, Sam, and Kyle pass. As Kyle wound the SUV up to the fourth and top level of the parking garage, Xander was numb. He'd been on these sorts of rides before. The rides where you're sure one of your own has just become one of the fallen. There was nothing else like it in the world. The silence in the truck said it all. Sam had been on these rides as well, and Kyle, well, he had sense enough to keep his mouth shut.

As they rounded the final turn up to the top of the parking garage, the afternoon sun welcomed them. Its light also bounced off a white sheet covering a gurney beside an ambulance at the edge of the garage. The shape of a body outlined beneath it. The very symbol of death. A life lost. Xander couldn't help but feel a member of Team Reign was gone.

A police officer waived Kyle over to a parking spot along the wall. There was yellow police tape everywhere. White cones marked spent bullet casings, and spatters of blood were scattered here and there on the light-gray concrete. Xander stepped out of the truck, and the heat brought a sickening feeling. It also opened a doorway in his mind, allowing past memories of days like this in, bringing him further heaviness. He ducked under the caution tape and walked the path around investigators busy trying to piece the scene together and directly over to the old man lying on a stretcher.

Jack removed his oxygen mask. "Xander. It's Zhanna."

Xander glanced over his shoulder at the body under the sheet. His heart dropped.

"They don't know if she's going to make it."

Xander whipped his head back over to Jack. "She's alive?" Hope had returned.

"She was when she left, but barely."

Xander finally exhaled. Hopefully she would be okay.

"The guy under the sheet there is who she saved me from. X, she jumped right in front of the bullet. Then took the guy down as she bled out on the concrete. She saved my life."

Xander patted him on the shoulder.

Jack hung his head. The naturally confident and charismatic old cowboy finally looked defeated.

"I'm sorry, Xander," Jack managed to say.

Xander asked the paramedics to give them a minute. The lines on Jack's face seemed deeper, the sorrow in his eyes, never-ending. "Are you all right, Jack?"

Jack looked up at him like he was crazy for asking such a thing. "Xander, Zhanna is—"

"I know, Jack. I asked about you."

Jack hung his head again. "I'm fine. It's just a damn flesh wound."

Xander looked up and found the face of the paramedic hovering nearby. The paramedic nodded as if to say he was telling the truth.

"This isn't your fault, Jack. It's mine."

"Son," Jack said, wincing as he shifted to face Xander, "I don't need hero talk right now. I've been in this game long enough. This ain't nobody's fault but ours for not watching our own backs. Which is my fault, cause I'm the senior here."

"We underestimated everything about this mission, Jack. And it might have cost Zhanna her life. This is on me."

"Yeah, well, you wasn't here," Jack said, his deep growl shaky. "We were put here to watch Sarah. Not only did we fail at that simple task, but we couldn't even watch ourselves. We're dealing with a different kind of animal here in Brancati, son. He's more than just a one-man band. You've gotta regroup and go after this guy in a different way. He's got the upper hand, you've gotta get it back."

Xander let go of Jack's hand. "That's the least of my worries, Jack. Right now I'm going to get you and Zhanna back to the States. That's what matters. You two aren't flying home alone."

"The hell you are." The steadiness in Jack's voice had returned. "This guy better be your only worry. Him and whatever the hell he's helping to keep secret. Surely I don't have to remind you that there are lives at stake here. Not just your own, but Sarah's, and obviously a lot more folks than that. Zhanna is hurt real bad. She was willing to die trying to keep people safe. You ain't gonna let her possibly *die* in vain. You're gonna get that sum bitch."

Xander stood silent. He knew Jack was right, but one of his own was quite possibly dying on the way to the hospital.

Sam stepped closer. "Jack is right, Xander. What happened to Zhanna only further clarifies—"

"Not now, Sam." Xander stopped her.

She didn't continue.

Kyle came up and put his arm around Xander. "I'm sorry, X. But Zhanna's going to be okay. She's tough as nails."

Xander didn't speak; he just patted his friend on the chest and exhaled his lingering anxiety. He squinted through the sun as he turned away from the three of them and stared at the outline of the body under the sheet. That could've been Zhanna. Still could be. Something wasn't making sense. Nothing was really, but especially the time line of things. He had no idea why Brancati was after him, that much was true. But the crazier thing about all of it was that Brancati was here in Venice, too, passing along information about a weapon. How he was involved in both killing a CIA agent and targeting Xander couldn't be a coincidence. But how were they connected?

As much as he wanted just to take a moment and think, all he heard in his head were Jack's words. "You ain't gonna let her possibly *die* in vain. You're gonna get that sum bitch."

Xander took a deep breath to quell the growing fury. None of this in Venice had ever been just about Alessio Brancati. They all knew he was guilty somehow, but this couldn't be all about him right now. Sarah's text saying there was a weapon being built was what they had to focus on. That was the real threat. That was what Zhanna would want them to focus on. Not revenge but the weapon—powerful enough to warrant this destruction, including the deaths of an American agent and maybe one of Xander's own. As he stared at the covered body, he knew this was about to become the biggest threat he'd ever faced. Zhanna's redemption lay in making sure this weapon didn't find its purpose. Though Jack and Sam might think differently, bringing Brancati to justice would have to wait.

As soon as he turned back to his team to give them his thoughts, his phone began to ring. He pulled it from his pocket and was surprised by the name on the caller ID.

Sarah Gilbright.

"Sarah? Are you all right?"

All three of them looked at Xander with concern.

"Alexander King."

Not Sarah. Instead, a man's voice. Heavy Italian accent . . . Brancati.

Xander didn't respond. He walked away from the others to the edge of the parking garage overlooking the lagoon. Water taxis and gondolas flooded the water below. In the distance, a large yacht was still anchored. Maragos. He knew, because Brancati was calling from Sarah's phone, that she was no longer aboard that vessel. Add another failure to the mission here in Italy. Xander wasn't sure if he would ever set foot in one of his favorite cities ever again after this debacle.

"Nothing to say? Okay, I will do the talking."

Xander almost threw the phone into the lagoon.

Brancati continued, "When they needed you most, you were nowhere to be found. That has to sting."

The rage was building. Not only had this man murdered an American operative and come after members of Xander's team, he was rubbing it in. This wasn't the side of things Xander was used to being on.

"Now, I have another of your American agents. You see, you are playing checkers, King, while I am playing chess."

Xander took a moment to breathe through the growing fury and turned his back on the lagoon. The scene of Zhanna throwing her body in front of Jack to save him played out in his head. He could hear what sounded like a plane coming from Brancati's end of the call. He turned back to look at the sun floating above the shimmering water. Things were bad, and his team had been put behind the eight ball from the moment they landed in Italy. But Xander was about to catch up. And if Maragos, Brancati, and whoever else was involved in this act of war gave him enough time, they were going to wish they'd kept after him until he lay dead here in Venice. The thought of Sarah being caught in the middle helped a leak of adrenaline drip inside his veins.

"I'm playing checkers, huh?" Xander said. "And you think I'm going to just let you get away with this, Brancati? You must not know your enemy as well as you think you do."

17

Now It's Personal

SARAH WATCHED as Brancati ended the call to Xander from her phone. She couldn't be sure what Xander had told him, but she was sure it wasn't a surrender. She also didn't know what Brancati meant when he told Xander, "When they needed you most, you were nowhere to be found." She felt absolutely helpless. All she could do was hope that everyone was all right. At first, when she handed over her gun to Brancati to keep him from shooting Andonios, she felt like she had failed. But she did all she could do. She wasn't able to get a lot of information to Xander in that text message, but she knew, for Xander and Sam, it would be enough.

At least, that is what she hoped.

"Where are you taking me?"

She had to say it loud enough for Brancati to hear her over the scream of the jet engines. They had just taken off, Venice growing smaller and smaller below her window. Andonios sat in the seat beside her, Brancati directly facing her.

Brancati tucked his black ear-length hair behind his ear and smiled. "We have to get Andonios here back to Athens. Then, if you like, you and I can go island hopping. I have been to Greece many times, I could show you its beauty."

Sarah folded her arms and sat in silence. This guy was a real arrogant prick. Totally full of himself. He wore that smug smile like a car salesman promising the deal of a lifetime.

"Is that a yes?"

Ugh.

Sarah turned her attention to the window. What the hell was she going to do now? And what the hell were they going to do to her? Brancati had already killed at least one American agent, so clearly death was a possibility for her. But when she handed over her weapon on the yacht, they let her live. Maybe they would use her as a pawn. If so, Xander was in trouble. If there was one thing Xander King would throw all caution to the wind for, it would be her. She watched him do it for Natalie in Paris, and she heard how far he went in Syria to free Sam from Sanharib Khatib. Perhaps her best bet for now would be to play a little mental warfare.

"You have made a major misstep keeping me alive," Sarah told Brancati. She could see Andonios's jaw hang open as he sat beside her. She uncrossed her arms and sat forward on the edge of her seat. "I know you think you are untouchable, Brancati, but you have no idea who you are dealing with."

"Funny, King just told me the same thing." Now it was Brancati who sat forward. "Yet I am the only one who accomplished any of their goals in Venice. He is the one who is going to be burying someone he cares about."

Sarah's stomach dropped, but she did her best not to display her shock. Maybe he was bluffing, or maybe someone was already dead. Xander would be devastated regardless, but if it was Kyle or Sam, he would be shattered.

Brancati held his smile wide. "So, tell me, where is my misstep?"

Sarah stamped down her discouragement and looked Brancati straight in his eyes. "You made it personal."

18

A Little Understanding

THE NEXT COUPLE hours were touch and go for Team Reign. After the call from Brancati, Xander was ready to run through walls to get to the end of whatever the hell they'd been swept up in. Now that Sarah had given them a general location, Greece, it was hard for Xander to pull back the reins long enough to make sure Zhanna was all right at the hospital. But he needed to be there at the hospital before the team moved on. And Sam needed some time to put her head together with Marv's on exactly where the best place to start in Greece would be.

As Sam took to her computer in a spare office space, the doctors worked their magic on Zhanna, and while Jack was getting patched up, Xander and Kyle had the waiting area pretty much to themselves. There were people there, but their conversations weren't a distraction as they were all speaking Italian.

"How you holding up?" Kyle asked Xander.

Xander opened his eyes, trying to clear his head of the

madness of the last day and a half, but there it was again running nonstop on the flat screen television fixed to the waiting room wall.

"Fuming."

Kyle nodded as he followed Xander's eyes to the television where a police officer was being interviewed in front of the police tape atop the parking garage. "I learned a lot at Camp Peary."

Xander sat up, giving his old friend his full attention. "Yeah?"

"Yeah. Obviously they taught me a lot more about tactics, implementation, and a lot of the history behind espionage and real-world scenarios. But what I didn't expect was how it would help me better understand you."

Xander smiled. "I'm pretty sure we are thick as thieves, my friend."

Kyle shook his head, serious. "Yeah, I don't mean in a buddy-buddy kind of way." Kyle shifted and looked at Xander. "Remember when you decided to leave Lexington and join the Navy?"

"Hard to forget. It kind of changed my life path a bit."

"Yeah, well, it changed mine too. When you left and I didn't see you for a while, you came back and you were different."

"Things have been different for me since my parents—since my mom was murdered."

"Yeah, but you were still Alexander. When you came back to Kentucky for the first time after your first tour, Xander had taken over."

Xander looked confused. "I don't understand."

"I'm not saying I lost my friend when you left. There was just a part of you I didn't understand when you got back. And when I started working with you, driving for you, and seeing you be so cool and calm in the most dangerous of situations, I couldn't wrap my mind around how that was possible."

"They put you through it at Camp Peary, huh?" Xander started to get it.

"Man, they didn't put me through it. They broke me." Xander had never seen Kyle like this. "I understand now that's what happened to you in the Navy. I feel like now I know you better. Now I know how you deal with crazy adversity and still keep your head. At first I thought the training was bullshit. I had learned from you, I figured what more could they teach me?"

Xander's smile returned. "They put you through the mind maze. Good. I would never have been able to give you that. I love you too much."

"It was awful. But I'm so glad I stuck it out. I'll be able to be a much better teammate to you and Sam now. I won't be a liability."

Xander didn't like that word. "Brother, your lack of experience might have been dangerous for you, and us at times, but you were *never* a liability. I don't know how you did as well as you did in some of the crazy situations I put you in. I could have never done what you did without my training. I admire your guts. And now I'm glad we have another level to our friendship."

Kyle smiled and sat back in his seat. Xander was happy for his friend. The kind of missions they went on and the kind of people they had to face in some of the darkest parts of this world were going to be a lot easier for Kyle to process now. And it couldn't have been better timing. He was going to need the very best of the newly trained Kyle in the days to come. Of all the things that were uncertain, that much he knew. The sense that they were about to face something far more terrifying than ever before was running all through him. He could feel it in his bones. And he didn't much like the feeling.

"I don't understand something," Kyle said.

Xander was so deep inside his own head he jumped when Kyle spoke.

"Yeah, which part?"

"When I was leaving Langley, Director Hartsfield pulled me into her office to brief me. She started with why you were going to Venice. American agent killed, you and the team trying to recover the information that made that happen. Standard stuff. So I get why we are after the flash drive and Brancati, but what I can't for the life of me understand is why in the hell is Brancati after you?"

19

Make It a Double

A LONG BLACK limousine with dark tinted windows came to a stop at the corner of Twenty-Eighth Street and Pennsylvania Avenue. It was springtime in Washington, DC, and the chill of the winter had finally begun to thaw. Just outside the Four Seasons Hotel the green was returning to the trees, and along the sidewalks, flowers were just beginning to bloom. None of which Senator Graham "Big Rig" Thomas gave one tiny little shit about. Wasn't his kind of thing. He'd acquired the nickname Big Rig when he was a linebacker for the Texas Longhorns. He was known for running over even the most stalwart of running backs. His six-foot-three, 240-pound frame made the epithet all the more sticky, and he carried the Big Rig nickname into his terms in the Senate, where he was known to run right over those who stood in his way there too. Though his dark hair had given way to white and wrinkles aged his rugged good looks, for the most part the senator had been able to maintain his intimidatingly charismatic presence.

He fingered the button on the door and the black window came down, letting in the last of the cool evening's light. He motioned out the window for the man standing on the corner to make his way to the car. He opened the door, left it ajar, and scooted over in the seat, leaving room for his old friend and fellow congressman, Jerry McDonnell, to join him.

"Jackson," Senator Thomas shouted to his driver, "take a walk."

Jackson didn't need clarification. He'd been on many walks around many blocks in DC as the senator conducted private business in the comfort of the back of his limo.

"Graham." Jerry, the tall and thin man, said hello as he shut the door behind him. The two men were alone in the large cabin of the vehicle.

"Jerry, would you like a scotch?" Graham asked as he poured himself one from a crystal decanter.

"Make it a double."

"Rough day?"

Jerry turned toward him, his wrinkled brow furrowed. "Cut the shit, Rig. Is this really necessary? We couldn't just discuss this over the phone?"

"You got something more important to be doing?"

"Unless we have a problem, yes. Marlene and I have theater tickets tonight."

Graham scoffed. "Theater tickets? I'm battling my ass off to keep us from spending the rest of our lives in jail and that's what you're worried about? The theater?"

Jerry's face changed from annoyed to concerned. "That's what I'm paying you to do. To worry about it. So I don't have to. So what's the problem, Rig? Did I make a mistake having you put this together? You said you had everything under control."

Graham handed Jerry his double scotch, and Jerry took it

down in one slug. Graham took a sip from his own glass and tried to calm the angry congressman. "I do have it under control. *Now.* Thanks to the relationship you told me to stay away from."

"She gave you information? You've got to be kidding me. That doesn't seem like something she would do."

Graham smiled. "I wouldn't use the word *gave.*"

"Well, whatever. How bad is it?"

Graham took another drink. "We're okay for now. Things got a little crazy in Venice last night. I'm not sure if you saw the news—"

"Oh, I saw it," Jerry broke in. "You're telling me that had to do with us? With what we're doing?"

"It's complicated, Jerry. But we have it under control for now. You ever heard of Alexander King?"

"Guy with the racehorses? Used to be a Navy SEAL or something?"

"Yeah, him."

"What about him?" Jerry said.

"He's the problem."

Jerry didn't say anything for a moment. He reached across Graham and poured himself another double. "I'm trying to make the connection here, old friend, but I don't get it. What's he have to do with any of this?"

"He's an agent of sorts for the CIA."

"King? How did you—"

"Don't worry about how I know. Point is, he was sent in to Venice to track down a flash drive that had some potentially devastating consequences to our little project."

Jerry's face scrunched, "You mean *my* little project. You may have found Gregor, but it's my money that is making this happen. And it's my money that will make you a billionaire when it works."

Graham let Jerry think he was still in charge. It worked better that way. If something went wrong, it further distanced Graham from being a part of it. Wouldn't be his money that would be traced. It would be Jerry's. Jerry always thought he was smarter than Graham.

"Yeah, that project, Jerry. Like I said, I'm working my ass off to make sure it doesn't get us both killed or sent to prison."

Jerry covered his face with both hands, rubbing, seemingly trying to wrap his head around this turn of events. He dropped his hands, and his face morphed back to annoyed.

"Get to the bad news then. So we're both in trouble? This King guy going to out us?"

"For now, we're okay. I'm doing damage control. But the information didn't get out. So we're good."

Jerry finished his drink and set his glass on the mobile bar. "What is the information, and how worried do I need to be?"

Graham finished his scotch and set down his glass as well. "You don't need to worry, I'm just keeping you informed. I have it all under control. Helps to be the smartest guy in the room once in a while. The information is that our project is complete. That son of a bitch Maragos pulled it off."

"You mean the nanobots? He got them up and running?"

"Making them by the dozens as we speak."

Jerry sat back and took a deep breath. Letting that sink in. "This is huge, Rig. You really buried the lead there."

"Massive," Graham agreed.

Jerry looked him in the eyes. "Okay, so what's the problem? What's the deal with Alexander King, and why does it matter?"

"Maragos went a little too far to make sure the information didn't get out."

Jerry looked at him, concerned. "What the hell happened, Rig?"

"Don't panic, 'cause like I said, I have it under control."

"I don't like the sound of this."

"Relax. An American agent was killed, but I—"

"An American agent? Killed? How will this not blow back on me?"

"Damn it, Jerry, I told you to relax."

Jerry's chest was heaving. "I knew I shouldn't have let you run this. I knew this Maragos guy was shady. Shit!"

He slammed his hands down on the black leather seat.

Graham gave Jerry a moment to settle down.

"So, what, now the CIA is going to find out everything? That I'm involved and ultimately responsible for the death of an American operative?"

"Not going to happen. Thanks to my date waiting inside, like I said, we were able to stop the information from getting back to the CIA. Our little problem in King is about to go away too. So don't worry about it. I'm just keeping you up to date."

Jerry put his hand on the door handle. "You keep saying don't worry about it, yet here I am. I'm not sure what you mean about King is about to go away too."

"Let's just say that someone better than him is going to make sure he doesn't interfere."

Jerry shook his head. "You'd better be right about that, Graham. Get it done. I don't care how it happens."

Graham opened his door and got out of the limo. Jerry followed suit, getting out the other side. Graham walked around the back of the limo, wearing a smile as he walked right past his old friend toward the Four Seasons entrance. "I'll just have your cut of the money wired to your offshore account when the sale goes through."

Jerry didn't respond.

Graham just kept walking.

Once inside the hotel lobby, Graham made his way over to the entrance to Bourbon Steak, his favorite restaurant in all of DC. He knew this was all just a minor setback. The important thing was that Gregor Maragos had held up his end of the deal and created the nanobots. Technology that scientists and journalists have been writing about would change the world of warfare for years, *if* someone could actually perfect it. Now that that had happened, and his shell company was first in line to purchase the technology (thanks to his connections in getting the materials to Maragos), his plan of getting ultrarich and exacting sweet revenge now lingered on the tip of his tongue.

Speaking of the tip of his tongue, he could already taste that juicy prime rib making his mouth water. He approached the hostess stand. Amy was working tonight.

"Hello, Amy."

"Hey there, Senator Thomas. Good to see you again. Your date is already seated. Follow me and I'll take you on back to her."

"Perfect," he said with a wink.

Perfect in many ways, in fact. As Amy walked him back to his table, he saw his beautiful date stand to greet him, and he knew that without her, the last twenty-four hours would have gone much different. And so would have his conversation with Jerry in the limo. He would never have known the US was sending Xander King to Venice. And he would never have been able to hire Alessio Brancati in time to stop him. Graham had never been more proud of himself for the way he'd been able to charm all this info out of her. Being good in bed had given him a fantastic opportunity. But he wasn't naive. He knew the Sodium Pentothal, aka "truth serum," that he had slipped into her wine before bed might have had something to do with it. The best part of all for Graham was that his date, Mary Hartsfield, *the* director of the CIA, had absolutely no memory of the conversation. It just made the high-powered woman as chatty as all the other women he'd ever slept with. The difference, and it was a lifesaving one, was that her pillow talk meant something. And he would be more than happy to steal a few more postcoital insider tidbits from her tonight. His bank account, and his life, might very well depend on it.

"There you are," Mary said.

Graham kissed her on the lips. "Sorry I'm late, honey. It's been a crazy day."

Mary took her seat and let out a long sigh. "Tell me about it."

Graham smiled all the way down to his rotten core. "That bad? You'll feel better if you get it off your chest. I always do. Besides, I'm a really good listener."

20

Try the Back Door

"AT LEAST I'M STILL ALIVE," Dbie said to the 431st successfully programmed nanobot of the night.

Alive and still working. The conversation in Gregor Maragos's office went absolutely as bad as it could go. But . . . her desperate attempt to make herself indispensable at the end proved to keep her alive. Sure, two Greek goons had been assigned to watch her back 24/7—she looked back over her shoulder and gave them a fake smile—and yes, she had to go directly to a solitary and fully monitored room in the warehouse now to live and sleep immediately after finishing her work for the day, but she was—for now, at least—alive.

A prisoner, but alive.

She really needed to work on a way to keep herself alive when she was finished. That's what she should really be focused on now. The minute she handed over enough bots, or the minute someone else came in that could do it instead of her, she was dead. Now *that* is a problem. One she had no idea how to manage. She was useless to Gregor once her tasks were completed. Flying these things once they were coded was a piece of cake. A nine-year-old in the back of a trailer with a Wi-Fi connection and an Xbox controller could do it.

The only resolution to the problem of dying after she finished was to, well, not finish. And that wasn't an option. If she refused to work or to train someone else, these were the kind of people who would find her mom, and her two-year-old golden retriever, and kill them both. So if not finishing wasn't an option, where did that leave her?

It was late in the warehouse and work time was over—well, over for everyone who wasn't trying to tell the United States about this operation—so the entire place was quiet. That's why it made her jump when she heard the door at the back of the warehouse slam. She jerked around nervously, half expecting to see Gregor coming with a gun pointed at her head, but her scanning eyes found no one. She turned back and looked down at her software program, the one she'd written herself to make these little bots do what she needed them to do.

It was then that an idea hit her like a bolt of lightning through a metal umbrella: she needed a *back door* of her own.

That slamming door just may have saved her life. *If* she could figure out a back door. And that was a big if. Doctor Kruger was checking up on her regularly as it was. Now that they knew she had tried to leak information, Kruger would be checking up on her even more. And though she didn't look it, Kruger was a smart woman. The question was, could she read code? Or would she, even if she could?

Dbie looked over her shoulder again. She was starting to feel suffocated by the Greek goon squad, but they had no idea what the hell she was doing on her computer. She may as well have been playing Donkey Kong. And Kruger was nowhere in sight, for now. Probably going down on the Dilbert look-alike in his office. Ew.

Dbie took a deep breath. She needed a clearheaded moment here. Her life hung in the balance . . . but did it? Did it really? She was a dead woman if she didn't try *something*. Nothing actually hung in the balance at all really. Doesn't that make the decision easy? She had no other choice. If she didn't create a way to make herself useful after the bots were finished, she would be the one who was finished. And she had a feeling a bunch of innocent people might be dead right along with her.

Time for a little construction. She logged back in to the nanobots' system on her laptop. She had to make these things work for Maragos now but give them a little bug of their own so they would get sick later, leaving her the only one who could make them better. Or at least leaving her some way to control them. This would ensure that she would remain indispensable, making her impossible to murder.

She typed away.

How does computer software have a back door, sweetheart?

As often happened when things got stressful, she heard her mother's voice. It wasn't as strong as it used to be, but neither was her mom. As usual, though, it helped her focus. And she didn't care if it made her sound crazy to talk back to her. It was only in her head, so that made it okay, right?

Hey, Mom. I miss you. Dbie spoke to her mother in her head as she began coding in the nanobots' system. *So, back door. You know how when I was young and we used to watch old* Mission Impossible *reruns on TV? Well, it's kind of like that. When Jim would play the tape giving him his mission, and then the tape would self-destruct when it had finished playing, that's what I am trying to do here. The back door I build in will give me a way to control, or malfunction, the nanobots. But I don't know if it will work, Mom. There is no way that I can test it now. Not while I'm being so closely watched. I'll just have to pray it works when the time comes, if I can even get access to their controls. If it does work, I'll have a chance to see you again. If it doesn't, then I've left you to fight your battle all on your own. And, icing on the cake, I might go down in history as the one responsible for unleashing these terrible things on the world. You know, Mom, no big deal.*

Dbie continued to try to set herself up to have some sort of a chance at survival. She let out a deep and woeful breath, sarcastically telling the Greek goons what she'd told her mother in her head . . .

"No big deal at all."

21

Too Easy

XANDER'S GULFSTREAM 650 private jet pulled its wheels into its undercarriage as it floated peacefully away from Venice, Italy. Xander had never been so happy to leave a place. Even though where he was going was flying right into all-out war, he couldn't for the life of him imagine how it could get worse than the last two days in the most romantic city in the world.

Nothing good happened in Venice, that much was certain. But at least Team Reign was leaving with all of its members still breathing. Jack would stay overnight to make sure he had no complications from his gunshot wound. And Zhanna, though she had a fight ahead of her, the doctors told them that they fully expected her to survive. The bullet had hit an artery in her left thigh, but Jack, though struggling through the pain of being shot himself, had saved her life by making a tourniquet with his belt just above her open wound.

Kyle, Sam, and Xander, the three musketeers left standing, were on their way to Greece to follow some leads that Sam had managed to uncover while waiting at the hospital. Xander passed Sam the last of the pasta they had picked up on their way out, the three of them finally having a proper meal.

"Okay, Sam," Xander said between bites. "Now that we've had time to settle in, let's get started. What's our first move?"

Sam chased her bite with a drink of water, pulled her tablet from her bag, and opened the file she'd been putting together.

"I've been doing some research on the Maragos brothers. We all know their story, inheriting their father's wealth and continuing his business affairs. Which are vast. I started by trying to locate facilities in their name. Places that could be large enough to build a weapon."

Kyle interrupted. "So we have no idea what kind of weapon, right?"

"Correct," Sam answered.

"So in theory, this weapon could be built in a garage, or a warehouse. So how does that help narrow things?"

"I agree. That is why I had Marvin look into the materials they have purchased over the last several months. If there are any new materials, especially some that don't fit their normal operations, that could be our first clue."

"Good thought." Xander took a bite of a buttery baguette. He hadn't really eaten in days, and it was hard not to shovel the food in.

"Right," Sam said. "It was a good thought. But Marvin's search didn't turn up any new materials coming into their facilities."

Kyle said, "Dead end number one."

"When one door closes . . . ," Sam said. She swallowed a bite of pasta. "While that didn't turn up a materials flag, it did lead Marvin to search for any other listed materials coming into Greece. There was a hit on a company called Rig's Recycling."

"That doesn't sound very Grecian," Xander said.

"No," Sam agreed. "And it is a newly formed company. So more than one red flag there."

"What do we know about it?" Kyle asked.

"They made several large purchases in the last twelve months. All of which seem to reflect a recycling business. There are a couple more real estate purchases that are ambiguous, and Marvin is looking into those as we speak."

"So who owns Rig's Recycling, and what does it have to do with the Maragos brothers?" Kyle asked.

Sam answered. "That's where it gets interesting. After catching Marvin's attention for the flagged materials, he found that the owner is a man called Theo Kyrkos."

"Doesn't really sound all that interesting," Kyle said.

"If you let me finish, it might." Sam shot him a killer look.

"Easy, you two, you were doing so well." Xander smiled.

Sam continued, not dropping her evil eye. "Theo Kyrkos, *Kyle*, is also listed as having his office at the new Rig's Recycling facility in Santorini, Greece. A facility that was previously owned by the Maragos brothers."

"Okay," Kyle conceded, "you have my attention."

"You ready for this? After a little more digging . . . Theo Kyrkos is married . . . Would you like to guess the maiden name of his wife Anastasia?"

"It can't be," Kyle sat forward.

"Yep, Maragos."

Xander set down his plate. "You have got to be kidding me."

"I'm glad I am not." Sam smiled.

"It can't be this easy," Kyle said, laughing.

"Why would they do that?" Xander asked. "Why would she *let* them do that?"

Sam said, "We can't be certain why they would do it, if it actually does have a connection to the weapon building, but I did find an article that may clue us in a bit."

"Do tell," Kyle said.

"The Maragos family is like royalty in Greece. Therefore, the press is always writing stories. I combed through at least a thousand of them, looking for something that may help us. At the time when I found an article titled "The Other Maragos" about the estranged daughter who disowned the royalty of her family, I didn't think anything of it. However, when Marvin told me about this connection, I thought maybe the brothers' motivation was if they ever did get caught, which clearly they are arrogant enough to think they never will, but if they did, maybe they would try to pawn it off on her?"

Xander thought about it for a minute while Sam poured some more water. It didn't make any sense to him at all. Why, if you were building something so sinister that it required killing an American agent to keep it secret, would you leave a glaring connection like tying someone with your famous last name to the paperwork? It was too easy. Someone smart enough to maintain an empire—and build weapons made for terrorism, if that's what this was— couldn't possibly be dumb enough to make this sort of error.

"We are missing something," Xander announced.

"We're missing a lot of things," Sam added. "Anything specific in mind?"

Xander rolled with a thought. "Do we have any idea just how estranged their sister is? Or if for sure she still is?"

"The article was written last year. That's all I've got. What are you thinking?"

"Well, there is just no way Maragos would leave a loose end like this blowing in the breeze for any half-cocked investigator to be able to tie him to."

"You don't know that," Sam said.

"There is just no way. Do some more digging on Rig's Recycling. Something's off."

"What are you thinking, X?" Kyle said.

"We are looking too narrow. We are making this all about the Maragos brothers."

Sam said, "That's because Sarah specifically told us that Gregor Maragos is building a weapon."

"I get that, Sam. But it was also a quick text before they took her phone. You don't think there is more to the story? How are they getting these listed materials? Who is helping them shade their movements? If they really do have the press on them all the time, someone or some corporation has to be helping them stay under the radar. And on top of that, don't forget, someone had to know that I was going to be in Venice. If you don't think these two things are connected, you are out of your mind."

Sam nodded. "That was my next order of business. And I agree with you, Xander. The coincidence is too strong, the two things must be connected. Whoever hired Brancati to come after you *must* be connected in some way to Maragos and what he is building. The difference between getting ahead of this thing and getting buried by it may very well lie in finding that connection."

"Do we have any leads, any ideas?" Kyle asked.

Everyone was quiet for a moment. The jet engines hummed. The black night outside the window was as vast as the gap seemed between what they knew and what they needed to know. Xander closed his eyes and let his mind wander over the situation. They knew Gregor Maragos was involved. Prime suspect number one. They knew Alessio Brancati was involved. Prime suspect number two. The deep gap in finding prime suspect number three lay in a few things. Who could somehow have known Xander was going to Venice? The list of people were on one hand, and he trusted all of them implicitly. He would have to circle back around to that later. Another starter for anything like this is motivation. Brancati's motivation was simple—pay him to do a job. More complicated was Maragos's motivation and unknown prime suspect number three's motivation. Most motivation has to do with one of two things: money or revenge.

In this particular instance, money, at least for Gregor Maragos, couldn't be the motivating factor. The guy was swimming in cash. So where could revenge come into play? They needed to know more about Maragos. More than just the surface. They needed an expert.

Xander's mind pinged on something. "Sam, who wrote the article about Maragos's estranged sister?"

The three of them snapped out of their silence and leaned back into the conversation. Sam picked up her iPad, swiped a few times, then zoomed in.

"Daphne Tomaras. Why?"

"We're heading to Santorini now, right?"

"Yes, to investigate the Rig's facility there."

"Fly Daphne to Santorini. I want to talk to her about the Maragos family. Tell her to bring all of her research about the family. Pay her whatever it takes to motivate her."

"You think she may offer something that can clue us in on Maragos's motivation, don't you?" Sam understood.

"You got it. Money and revenge, Sam."

"And Maragos doesn't need money," Kyle said.

Xander smiled. "Maybe they actually taught you a few things at Camp Peary."

"What are you hoping to hear?" Sam asked Xander.

"Maybe somewhere in the family history there is a reason Gregor Maragos is mad at the world. Or mad enough at someone in particular to build a weapon to attack them. I'm guessing so. In the meantime, as I'm sure you already are, follow the money on Rig's Recycling. There has to be a clue as to who really set this company up."

Sam put away her iPad. "Already have Marvin on it."

"Great, see you in Santorini."

Xander swiveled his chair and closed his eyes. Though he would make an effort to sleep, sleep would not come. The only thing Xander could do was picture Sarah in trouble. After that, for the entire hour left before they landed in Santorini, all he saw was Alessio Brancati's face.

Sleep doesn't come easy when your blood is set to boil.

22

Xander King Is a Problem

"WE'VE GOT A MINOR PROBLEM."

Gregor held the phone away from his ear, took a breath, and awaited the bad news from his unlikely partner.

"You there?"

Gregor sighed. "Yes, Senator Thomas, I'm here. But I've got no time for any more problems."

"Like I said, minor. You just keep doing what you're doing and I'll handle it," Graham reassured him.

Gregor never liked this man. Typical American arrogance and overconfidence. But as with a lot of things in life, events bring people together, and what happened to Gregor's father fortuitously brought Senator Graham Thomas and himself a common enemy.

"What exactly is the problem?" Gregor asked. "Your man was able to secure the flash drive as you said he would. He brought some unwanted attention from your government, but it seems we have it handled. And it actually produced a mole that had been infiltrating the family through my brother."

"Wait, what?"

Gregor could tell that Graham was surprised.

"That's right," Gregor continued. "Whoever your source in your intelligence community is, they have more information than you think."

"My source is the only reason we still have a shot at this. Hell, besides me, she's the only one in the entire government who has the information I have."

Gregor laughed. "Well, I now have information that you don't. A woman, Sarah Gilbright, is on her way here with my brother and your hired man, Brancati. Brancati says she is an American operative."

"I don't know the name. But that can only be good for us in case things get hairy."

"I'm assuming things won't, that's why I have you, remember?"

Graham cleared his throat. "I hear you. I'm on it. The only thing you need to know is to stay buttoned up. We can't afford to have your location compromised. The man on your heels now, well, let's just say he isn't the type to miss his mark all that often."

"Seems he missed just yesterday in Venice."

"Yeah, thanks to me and the info I extracted from my source. Otherwise, King would have had your flash drive already, and probably your head. I'm telling you, don't mess around with this guy."

Gregor felt everything closing in on him. Dbie Johnson had really mucked up everything with his time line. For the first time, he was beginning to regret killing Doctor Birschbach. Birschbach would have been able to finish Dbie's work. She should be the one dead. His next thought brought him focus: if he wanted to succeed with his mission, the past needed to stay in the past. He needed to act with only the next few crucial days in mind.

"So what do you plan to do about this *problem?*" Gregor said.

"You said Brancati is almost to you, correct?" Graham asked.

"Yes."

"Good. Tell him I will have Xander King's whereabouts in just a little bit. I am with my source now."

The senator sounded confident. Gregor didn't know how the American was getting this top secret information, but he really didn't care. That's one of the many reasons the pair of them had come together.

"I need something else from you, Senator."

"I'll do what I can."

"I need more information on this Xander King and whoever he might have working with him. I trust you will handle it, but I always like to have a backup plan. Especially with the stakes being so high."

"Like I said, I'll do what I can, but I can't promise that. The way I get my information is a touchy situation. If I press my luck, it might bring everything down on us. What exactly are you wanting?"

Gregor covered the phone and asked Doctor Kruger what she needed from the senator. He relayed what she told him to Graham. "All I need is their cellular phone numbers."

Graham laughed. "Oh, is that all? I don't think you realize exactly what a Black Op is, Maragos. I'm not even supposed to know Xander exists in the world of espionage. If I wasn't banging the only human on earth who knows about him, we'd have nothing. No way she's going to give me that info. No shot."

Gregor thought for a moment. He had an assembly of some of the best technological minds on the planet working right there in his facility. And his all-star hacker, Dbie Johnson, owed him a huge favor as it was.

"I understand the sensitivity of the information you've been able to procure. Just get her to give me names. I'll be able to do the rest."

"No promises. But that doesn't need to be the focus anyway," Graham said. "I need to know how close you are to your goal on the nanobots? Because a lot of things could go wrong here. I really think we need to move up the schedule. Now."

"I don't like changing plans. But . . . I agree with you. I don't like the way things are going. The problem is, if I am ready today, that throws off our time line and we will have to rework our execution timing."

"You let me worry about what happens once you bring those things to US soil, Maragos."

Gregor rubbed the bridge of his nose for a moment. He was putting a lot of trust in someone he didn't know. If it wasn't for the fact that their reasons for being in this were tied so strongly, he would never disrupt a well-laid plan. Especially just because some half-wit American soldier was sniffing around.

"All right, Senator. We have plenty of bots ready for our task. Especially since we really only need one."

"Okay, I'll get things ready. It's late Saturday here in DC. Can you be here ready to go by Monday afternoon?"

"That where he is going to be?"

"It is. And it sure would be a damn shame if he suffered some strange disease from a damn mosquito bite."

Gregor could hear the smile as Graham spoke those last words. He looked up to see his own reflected in the mirror across his desk.

"A shame indeed."

23

A Spy Movie's Favorite Cliché

THIS WAS DEFINITELY a first for Sarah. She'd been on many dangerous cases with the FBI, followed by a lull in action when she first joined the CIA. After she crossed paths with Xander King, things got kicked up a notch. She was involved in shoot-outs in Moscow and Tuscany and an all-out terrorist war in Paris, where there were several moments she was sure she wasn't going to live. But never before had she been driven to a remote area with a bag over her head. Every spy movie's favorite cliché. Unfortunately, this was no movie. This danger was real.

Other than knowing she was in Athens, Greece, she had no clue where they were taking her. She assumed it would be for a face-to-face with Gregor Maragos so he could see just what level of information she knew exactly. She knew he never liked her ever since Andonios first started bringing her around. When you're building an illegal weapon, naturally your suspicions are high. But now that her cover was blown, she figured there was little chance she would survive this. She assumed what little time left they gave her would only be to find out more about Xander and how close he was to closing in on them. Other than the rumble of the street below the vehicle, a sense of impending doom was all she felt.

Xander would know to come to Greece since she'd told him it was Gregor building the weapon. But how would he ever find where she was? Especially with absolutely zero time to spare. Sam was good, but not even she could figure something like this out so quickly. Not even with Marvin's help. If Sarah had any shot of getting out of this, she was going to have to do it herself.

The car came to a stop and the door opened. A wave of warm humid air came in to greet her. So did an overly aggressive hand around her right bicep, yanking her from the back seat. She would normally fight the man off, but her hands were bound by a plastic zip tie. Another hand wrapped around her other arm, then two men escorted her inside. No one said a word. The only sounds were muffled, some sort of machine cutting metal. The change in temperature after the door closed behind her was stark and gave her a chill. She had no sense for what kind of building she was in. After a few more open doors the two men released her into a room and shut the door behind her. She could tell that a light was on, but not much else. That is, until she made out a tiny bit of movement directly in front of her.

Sarah put her hands up in defense. "Don't come near me, whoever you are."

"Well . . . this can't be good," she heard a woman say. An American woman. "Close your eyes, this is going to be bright."

Sarah did as the woman asked. The bag was shimmied off her head, and she slowly opened her eyes, blinking in the light to give her eyes a chance to adjust. The woman cut her hands free of the zip ties.

"Who are you?" Sarah asked.

She was looking at a young woman. Dark brown hair pulled

back into a ponytail. High cheekbones below hazel eyes that were squinting inquisitively at Sarah's forehead.

"You're bleeding a little."

"Yeah. The boys weren't exactly gentle when they took my gun from me."

Sarah didn't understand why, but the woman's face turned sorrowful.

"Is this my fault?" the woman asked Sarah.

"I'm sorry. I just got brought here from the airport with a bag over my head. Can we rewind a bit? What's your name?"

"Oh, sorry." The woman wiped her hands on her jeans, then reached one forward. "I'm Dbie. Dbie Johnson. Are you all right?"

Sarah shook her hand and tucked her tousled hair back behind her ear. "Sarah Gilbright. I'm—"

Before Sarah could finish introducing herself as CIA, Dbie put her hand up as if to say stop, seemingly shielding it with her body. Then she held up a "wait a minute" index finger, mouthed the word "camera," and thumbed in the direction behind her. Sarah didn't have to look. She liked this woman already.

Sarah continued in a different direction. "I'm sorry I don't feel much like talking at the moment. I'm fine, but I'm a little shook up and a lot exhausted. Can I just have a few to collect myself? Then I want to know all about where we are and what is going on. I just can't think straight right now."

Dbie gave a hidden thumbs-up, then made a writing motion like she was moving an invisible pen. Sarah knew she meant she would write it down.

"Of course," said Dbie. "There is plenty to talk about, but it doesn't look like we're going anywhere anytime soon."

Sarah knew their audible conversations would all be surface from then on. She was anxious to read what the hell was going on, so she was hoping Dbie would get to it immediately. In the meantime, Sarah needed a plan.

24

Truth Serum

GRAHAM OPENED the door to his home. It wasn't far from the Four Seasons Hotel where he and Mary Hartsfield had just enjoyed a delicious dinner. As he anticipated, Mary offered no information during dinner, which confirmed that the Sodium Pentothal he had administered in her drink a couple nights ago had indeed done the trick. It was time for round two. The operative she had sent in to Venice could not be allowed to be a distraction or any kind of interruption going forward. The stakes were much too high.

"Let me take your coat," Graham, the gentleman he was, told Mary. "Still a bit of chill in the air, huh?"

"There is, and thank you." Mary handed over her coat and took a seat in the oversize brown leather chair. "I like what you've done with the decor. Very manly, but still stylish."

Mary was speaking of the rustic accents Graham had

installed. Lots of grey and rustic dark woods, accented by copper and modern lines.

"Thank you. I'd take credit, but my interior designer told me this is what was in. I like it, so it was fine. Listen, I still need to unwind a bit, I'm going to pour some scotch. Would you like some wine?"

"Got anything stronger besides scotch?"

"Of course. Gin martini?"

"Fancy."

Graham laughed. "Not really. But I make a good one."

"Sounds great. Hey, you mind if I space out on my phone for just a few minutes. Some really important things are going on and I can't miss them. I didn't mean to come back here and work, though, so if you prefer, I can head home. This just has to be done."

Graham walked over to the bar. "You kidding me? If anyone understands the call of work, it's me. I'll keep you company. If you don't mind."

"Sounds perfect. I won't be long."

"Take your time."

Take your time indeed. Graham poured his scotch and took a sip, smiling to himself. He began to make the martini. A perfect drink for what he needed to do, because the vial of truth serum was sitting right beside the olive sticks in the bar's top drawer.

Graham spoke with his back to the living room. "So, I know you said it's been a rough day. Anything we American citizens should be concerned with?"

Mary sighed. "Oh, you know, another day, another someone looking to burn America all the way to the ground."

Graham finished shaking the "truth serum" gin martini, poured it in a glass, and brought both drinks over to the living room. Mary was pecking away at her phone. She stopped long enough to take the glass. Drink up Ms. CIA.

"I can't even imagine the things you see and hear. Must be

hard to leave it at work," Graham said, beginning to peel the onion.

Mary eyed her oversize martini glass. "If I didn't know any better, Mr. Senator, I would think you were trying to get me drunk."

"Just sounded like your day deserved a double," Graham winked.

Mary returned the wink with a smile and took a long drink, draining almost half. "Wow, this is good. If they vote you out next term, at least you could still make a living."

"Silver linings." He smiled.

Mary went back to her phone.

Graham pressed. "Speaking of, are there any silver linings at all with what's going on right now? I heard about what went down in Venice. Some are rumbling it was our guys. But you know how that goes. The media is always speculating on things they know nothing about."

Mary looked up from her phone. "I can speak freely here, right?"

Graham couldn't contain a smile. This was exactly how she began when she opened up about sending Xander King into Venice the other night. This confirmed two things. She doesn't remember telling him about Venice, and the truth serum actually does work.

"Of course. You know I would never speak of anything we say here. I'd get in just as much trouble as you."

Mary took another drink. "I'm not sure that's true, but I get what you mean."

"So I take it Venice *was* an American operation."

Mary finished tapping on her phone's screen, took one more drink, then set them both down. "Sort of. It's complicated."

"It usually is." Graham acted like he was trying to relate, though at this point he could see by the glazed look in her eyes he didn't have to. That stuff worked fast. "How bad is it?"

"Bad."

There was no hesitation. Graham braced himself for her next words. They could very well be the difference between billions or life in prison, or worse.

"Nuclear bad?" he said.

"That part is unclear, but it very well could be."

Graham tried to sound shocked. "You mean that literally?"

"I'm getting ahead of myself, but there is something in the way of a weapon being—"

Mary stopped abruptly. Graham wasn't worried. She did this last time as well.

She continued, "Why am I telling you this? It—maybe I should go."

"Nonsense, Mary. It's fine. I don't mind. Probably good for you to talk about it. They say it's terrible for you to keep things bottled up."

Come on, old girl. Stay with me here.

"It's not that, it's just . . ."

"I know, it's sensitive information. I deal with it every day on the Hill."

Mary picked up her drink, took a sip, set it back down. Then she nodded. "I just haven't been director long, and I thought . . . I don't know what I thought really. I guess I figured I'd get to settle in a little more before something this big—globally big went down."

Graham swallowed hard. He needed to find out what they knew, right now, and get ahead of this thing.

"Wow, sounds like all the gin in the world won't help. You have a team ready for such an event?"

"The best we've ever had."

Graham tried to swallow again, but this time he couldn't. His mouth had gone dry. He wet it with the rest of his scotch. He knew Xander King was good, Mary had said as much last time, but the confidence in the way she said "the best we've ever had" fried his nerves completely. He steadied himself. "Well, that's good. They still in Venice?"

"Greece," Mary said as she came to the bottom of her martini.

Graham's stomach turned. He was finished. His heart was pounding. "Greece? You would think Russia or somewhere in the Middle East. Or hell, North Korea even."

"Right? No, the weapon is being built in Greece. Some dead rich guy's adult kid with a chip on his shoulder and not enough hugs."

Graham was going to throw a laugh out there for her, but he couldn't. So the CIA knew where and who. He needed to get word to Maragos immediately. If King was in Athens, he would shut this down before they could reap the benefits of any of the long process they had already gone through. No money, no revenge. Maragos would turn on Graham in a heartbeat, and Graham knew it.

He tried to recover. He needed more information. "So you'll be able to stop it then, if you know who and where."

"I wish it were that easy. This guy's family owns a lot of businesses. We're not sure exactly where he is. But I feel we don't have a lot of time before we *have* to know."

A glimmer of hope.

"What part of Greece?" Graham asked.

"Ah, top of my bucket list. Santorini. You ever been?"

The only thing Graham heard was Santorini. His shell game of buying up warehouses in different locales had paid off. They must have followed the materials trail to the recycling company he had set up. He'd hoped they would never get that far, but they did. And now he was feeling particularly proud of himself for the extra layer of separation he had put between himself and the company. There is no question they traced the ownership paperwork back to Maragos's sister. That's why they were headed there. He knew if they saw Maragos's last name tied to the owner as his wife, they would stop searching there. He'd kept himself in the clear. If he could stay there until Monday, he would send Brancati in to remove Gregor, leaving Graham and his old friend Jerry the trillion-dollar technology and no one to keep them from selling it. And better yet, no one to turn them in.

"Graham, have you been to Santorini?" Mary asked again.

Graham snapped back from his self-congratulatory moment. "I haven't, but I hear it's beautiful. Would you excuse me for just a moment? Too much water at dinner."

"Of course. And bring me another martini on your way back, if you don't mind."

Graham was already halfway to the restroom. Already dialing his on-call hitman too. The phone began to ring in his ear.

"Everything is under control." Such a slimy Italian accent.

"Save it, Brancati. It's only under control because I have it that way. You let Xander get away. And—"

"Yes, but I stopped the information from getting out."

"Bullshit!" Graham shouted. Then he lowered his voice so Mary wouldn't hear. "The hell you did. The CIA knows about the weapon, and they know about Maragos."

Silence.

"What, nothing to say, you arrogant prick?" Graham was tired of having to keep this together all by himself.

"Watch who you are talking to, Mr. Thomas. I am not the man you want upset with you."

"Whatever. I'm going to do most of your job for you. King and his team are headed to Santorini. They think that is where Maragos and the weapons are. Take him out there and I'll double what I'm paying you. I need him to go away."

"Consider it done," Brancati said with confidence.

"I'll send you the address of the warehouse he is going to be looking at. Take him out there. Then we can talk about what's next. But nothing happens until King is out of the picture. That clear?"

"I told you it will be done. Have your money ready, Signor Thomas."

Graham ended the call. As bad as things had become, he'd managed to stay on top of it. It's how he worked. Now it was time to see if there were any other secrets Mary had for him before the serum wore off. Specifically the names of the rest of Xander King's team. He didn't know why it mattered to Maragos, but he didn't much care either. Hell, the way the Sodium Pentothal had been working, he'd probably be able to get Mary to tell him if there really were aliens in Area 51 before the night was over.

25

Good News Travels Fast

THE SUN WAS RISING up the back side of the calderas—the mountainous rock formations that ancient volcanic eruptions had left sticking up from out of the sea—that made up the island of Santorini, Greece. Xander, Sam, and Kyle had just ordered breakfast and were awaiting the arrival of Daphne Tomaras, the reporter who jumped at the chance to share her knowledge of the Maragos family. For a hefty price of course. Just a couple of hours ago, before they went to bed for a short sleep, Sam was communicating with Marvin and texting with Director Hartsfield. Marvin was sure that this Rig's Recycling company was a sham, but the money was well tied off, and the only lead was the one they already had—that Gregor's brother-in-law, Theo Kyrkos, was where all the paperwork led back to. Xander and crew found this to be about as fishy as the Aegean Sea surrounding the caldera they were dining on. They needed something to pan out with this reporter. Potential information from her and visiting Kyrkos at the recycling facility were their only options. Sam was looking into finding Kyrkos's home address, just in case Kyrkos wasn't at the facility, and maybe they would actually get to speak with Maragos's estranged sister as well. Hardly worth crossing fingers there.

"So what is our goal here?" Kyle asked.

"To see if you can actually eat all three of those plates of food," Xander joked. "The CIA not feed you at Camp Peary?"

"The food there was fine. I'm just eating my feelings. Sam dumping me has really taken an emotional toll."

Sam didn't so much as look up from her plate.

Xander smiled at his friend.

"What?" Kyle said, looking over at Sam. "Too soon?"

"Just eat your bloody food." Sam shot him a look.

Xander made an "ooh, she showed you" face to Kyle.

"Fine." Kyle gave in. "No fun. I get it. So answer my question then. What's our goal with this reporter?"

"This is her walking up now," Sam said, rising from her seat. Then to answer Kyle, she continued, "Clueing in on Gregor's father is our goal. Maybe something about his death will tell us something about Gregor's motivation."

A short, dark-haired, olive-skinned young woman approached the table. She nodded to Sam when Sam raised her hand to draw her attention. She looked as if she hadn't slept, probably because Xander had paid her extra to leave in the middle of the night.

Sam greeted her with a handshake. "Ms. Tomaras, thank you for coming on such short notice."

"Pleased to meet you." Her English was good.

Sam introduced everyone, and they all took their seats. Everyone except for Daphne.

"Is there a problem?" Sam asked.

Daphne just held out her hand.

"Right to it then." Sam reached into her back pocket. She

pulled out an envelope full of cash and placed it in Daphne's hand.

"Sorry," Daphne said, checking the envelope, smiling, then putting it away and taking her seat. "Can't be too careful. I've been burned a few times in situations like this."

Xander said, "So you get paid ten grand and flown private to Santorini often, do you?"

Daphne smiled. "No, I guess not."

"We don't have a lot of time, Ms. Tomaras," Sam said, jumping in. "We need to know everything you know about Leo Maragos and his last few months alive. Not the newspaper version. The version you weren't able to print."

"Can I ask why you want to know this, and who this is for?"

Sam said, "No, and no."

Daphne looked to Xander and Kyle. They both gave a closed-mouth smile.

"Okay. Not important, I guess." Daphne pulled a manila folder from her briefcase. "A lot of the media, which was a total shit-show when Leo Maragos killed himself, wrote the same story . . . your standard 'money can't buy you happiness' and 'it really is lonely at the top' articles. But I had been around Leo a lot in my first few years. The Maragos family was my only assignment." Daphne looked at Sam. "I'm sure you understand. It's the same way with the royal family in Britain."

Sam nodded.

"I got to know Andonios in particular. His playboy exploits were my main focus for a while. He let the media stay close because he loved the attention. After his father died, his drunken conversations would often turn into talks about missing his father, and quite often he would mention a particular deal that went sour right before his father killed himself."

This piqued Xander's interest. This was exactly the sort of thing he was hoping for. It didn't mean they'd found something, but dead deals that lead to billionaire suicides would piss off an impressionable son quite a bit. For Xander himself, though his own father didn't kill himself, it was of course his parents' deaths that sent him off to the Navy for revenge. Why wouldn't it affect Gregor Maragos the same way?

"Coffee?" Xander said. When Daphne nodded, he poured her a cup. "Tell us more about this deal."

"Well, I guess it never was a deal, actually. Leo Maragos was cut out just before everything went through."

Xander said, "What was the company?"

"It's been sold a couple times since this all went down. It was shady at best. But you will know the company. The media reported that Everworld Solutions was set to do a deal with Maragos, buying up a lot of his facilities."

Alarm bells went off in Xander's head the moment he heard the company's name. Though he didn't follow business news much, he'd heard the name of the company several times because the current President of the United States was the man who founded it.

Interesting.

Xander helped Kyle and Sam get up to speed. "Everworld Solutions was founded by President Williams."

Shocked would be the best way to describe Sam and Kyle's reaction.

"Yeah," Xander said. This was getting interesting indeed.

Daphne continued, "According to mainstream news, the deal just fell through, but Everworld Solutions had found several instances where Leo Maragos had purchased a lot of his land for facilities illegally, and they managed to buy them up out from under him through loopholes in the legal system. Which in turn hurt Leo's company's profits, and the stock plummeted."

Daphne paused to sip her coffee.

Xander filled the dead air. "But . . ."

"But," Daphne continued, "according to off-the-record Andonios, it was much more shady. He claimed that one of the officers, or someone in the company, planned the entire thing. He never thought it was your President that did this. But his weirdo brother, Gregor, apparently did."

That's all Xander needed to hear.

"Thank you, Daphne. This was very helpful. If you'll excuse us, we have to get going."

Xander stood, and Kyle and Sam followed.

"Wait, that's it? That's all you want?"

Xander smiled. "Enjoy Santorini, Ms. Tomaras. We have to go."

Xander walked away in a hurry. Sam and Kyle quickly caught up.

"Sam, get me on the phone with the President."

She had her ear to the phone. "Already working the channels."

"Kyle," Xander said, "call Marvin and tell him to send me a list of all the officers attributed to Everworld Solutions in 2011."

"Okay, but what am I missing here?"

"Just get me that list. Gregor Maragos's beef is with President Williams. Gregor thinks President Williams did his father wrong."

Kyle said, "So you think whatever weapon is being built is going to be used on the President?"

"I don't think it, I know it."

"Then why is the rest of the list important?"

"Kyle, I know President Williams."

Xander and his team saved the President's daughter in Paris just last year. He and Xander had stayed in contact ever since.

"He wouldn't conduct business this way. Daphne said that Andonios didn't think it was the President who was responsible for harming Leo's company. That it was someone else in the company. I remember seeing in the news when President Williams was running for office that his old company Everworld Solutions was being investigated for how it got sold and why."

The three of them reached their rental car. Xander got in the passenger seat, Sam got in back, and Kyle got in to drive.

Xander continued, "They never found anything shady on President Williams, just that he sold the company to distance himself from the controversy. I remember he had fired a few people before he left, but nothing ever came out naming anyone for anything specific. A lot of people on the board lost a lot of money because of how quickly and publicly President Williams left."

Kyle started the car. "I'm not a businessman, X. Help me out with where you're going with this."

"If Andonios is right, and someone on the board was under-cutting President Williams, by *stealing* Leo Maragos's assets, you know the President and that board member had to have it out. And whoever it was, he had to have lost a ton of money because of the way the President exited."

Kyle said, "I still don't get it."

"President Williams cost this board member a lot of money. Giving said board member a score to settle with the President."

"Xander." Kyle was getting impatient. "What does this have to do—"

"Rig's Recycling, Kyle. I told you on the plane that something was missing. Gregor Maragos is getting help. And a man high up enough in business could be the only fit to be able to get Gregor listed materials on the down low. Whoever President Williams pissed off on his own board of directors shares the same vendetta as Gregor Maragos. They both want payback on our President. The kicker is, I have a feeling this board member is using Gregor's estranged sister and her husband's name on all the recycling company's paperwork to tie it off solely on Gregor. Keeping this board member anonymous, and one smart son of a bitch."

Kyle finally caught up. "We find the board member, we find who's helping to build the weapon with Gregor Maragos. Then we can make him tell us about the weapon and stop it from being deployed."

"Bingo," Xander said. "Sam, how's it coming?"

"It's the middle of the night in the US, Xander. This will take a minute to clear a call. Mary Hartsfield isn't answering her phone at the moment. I don't have a way to call the President directly. She's our only way to him."

"Damn it!" Xander slammed his hand on the dash. "I don't care if the President is on top of the first lady right now. Get him on the phone! This doesn't just affect the President. Sarah's life is also on the line."

"I'll keep trying."

"Where to right now?" Kyle asked.

Sam handed her iPad to the front seat. It already had the GPS route dialed in. Kyle pulled out of their parking spot. "On it. Is this the Rig's Recycling warehouse?"

Xander had calmed himself. He knew it wasn't Sam's fault. But the President's life and the life of someone he loved possibly hanging in the balance would make any man's blood pressure rise.

"Yes," he said. "We need to talk to Theo Kyrkos. Then maybe we can really start to piece this thing together."

"God help us," Sam chimed in from the backseat.

"And doesn't Director Hartsfield *always* answer?" Xander asked.

"This is the first time she hasn't when I've called."

"Shit. Get someone over to check on her ASAP. The last thing we need right now is to lose our only connection with government clout."

26

Shell Game

KYLE PULLED in to the parking lot of the Rig's Recycling facility. At least that's what the GPS told them. By looking at the exterior of the building, you would never know what it was used for. There wasn't a sign to be found, and the parking lot was empty, save for two vans at the far end.

"Either we're early, or this place is no longer in business," Kyle said.

The three of them exited the vehicle. Xander walked over to the glass door. When he looked inside, there was a man sitting at a greeting kiosk. Xander opened the door and waved Kyle and Sam inside.

"Someone's here at least. Let's see what we can find out."

They walked inside. There was no decor to speak of. Just concrete floors and white painted walls. The man behind the desk stood when they walked in.

"Do you speak English?" Xander asked.

The man nodded. His dark hair was tousled, his demeanor reserved. Or was it . . . nervous?

"We'd like to speak with Theo Kyrkos, please."

"Um. Sure. I'll be right back, okay?"

Definitely nervous. The man walked through the door behind him, and Xander slid his hand to the grip of his Glock 19 resting at the small of his back. Kyle noticed this and reached for his own. Sam already had her pistol in hand.

She looked over at the two of them. "Glad to see we're all on the same page."

"Something's not right—"

Xander was about to suggest that they leave, but before he could speak the words, gunfire blasted and bullets sprayed through the glass door the man had just left through. The three of them dove behind the kiosk, readied their weapons, and prepared for a fight.

Sam was first to raise up and return fire after the gunshots stopped on the other side of the door. Xander slithered around the corner of the kiosk. Movement through the door caught his eye, and he fired a couple shots into the darkened room. His biggest concern in the heat of the moment was someone coming up behind them. He scooted away from the kiosk, told Sam with two fingers to his eyes, then pointing them outside, that he was going to check there. She nodded and fired again into the room, keeping whoever was on the other side at bay. Kyle took up Xander's position near the kiosk, and Xander stayed low as he ran out the door into the rising heat of the warm Santorini morning.

As he sidled up to the edge of the building, he was trying to focus his racing mind. Yet again, someone had the jump on them. And he couldn't imagine it was anyone but Brancati. And there was only one way he could know where Xander was going to be: a mole. Somewhere among the few who knew of Team Reign, someone was leaking information. But that would have to wait.

He would have to force it from his mind. Brancati warranted every last bit of Xander's attention.

Xander poked his head around the corner. The long side of the aluminum building stretched in front of him. Gunfire continued inside, but Xander saw no one. There was a collection of dumpsters off to the right of the building, about halfway down. He raised his Glock in front of him and raced for the dumpsters. Halfway there someone stepped out around the corner and fired a string of automatic bullets his way. He dove headfirst to the grassy patch behind the dumpster as the bullets clanged against the metal on the other side. He immediately bounced up to a crouched position, pressed his back against the dumpster, and waited.

The second he heard the swapping of a magazine, Xander eased around the corner of the dumpster. There was a dent in the white aluminum siding of the building. Before he dove behind the dumpster, it registered that the dent was about head high on the man shooting at him. Xander found the dent as he peered over the nose of his pistol, moved just to the right, and at the first sign of the first hair on the man's head moving back out to shoot, Xander squeezed the trigger twice. The man dropped to the ground, the blood from his head now splashed against that dent.

Xander moved toward the body in a crouch, his Glock still extended. He heard more gunfire as he eased open the back door. He poked his head inside, and two bullets bored into the metal door, just above him. He fired back two shots, but all he could see was the blur of a man running through a door on the opposite side of the building. Xander tried to catch up to him, still aiming his pistol back outside, but had to recoil when a couple more shots were fired in his direction. All he managed to see was a figure taking cover behind a red sports car. Then he heard its engine fire up.

Brancati.

27

A Note of Confidence

SARAH GASPED and sat straight up. For a moment she was confused; then it became clear once again exactly where she was. Still trapped in a small room in Athens, Greece.

A hostage.

She looked over to where Dbie had been sleeping. Nothing but an empty bed. They had never gotten a chance to talk. Or the chance to pass a note. Sarah was completely in the dark. No new information. She assumed this was where they were building the weapon, or weapons, whatever the case may be. She wished she could somehow get word to Xander to come to Athens.

Sarah moved to the edge of the small cot, took her face in her hands, and gave a rub. She had checked the door before falling asleep, making sure it was locked. There was nowhere for her to go. She hoped Dbie was okay. Sarah believed Dbie that she was a prisoner herself; otherwise, she would have been prodding her for information. She was surprised that no one had come and talked to her. She couldn't decide if that was good or bad. She hoped good. Maybe the shit was hitting the fan and they were scrambling.

Sarah went to lean back, and as her hand moved under her pillow, it grazed something that felt a lot like a sheet of paper. Sarah glanced up at the camera fixed to the corner of the white cinderblock room. She stretched her arm, then made it look like she was turning over, back to the camera, for some more sleep. She slowly pulled the sheet of paper from under her pillow, keeping her body between it and the camera. It was clearly from Dbie. What a huge risk to slip this under her pillow. She hoped it wasn't why she was missing from the room this morning. She hoped Dbie was all right.

Sarah read the note:

I was the woman who reached out for help from the US government. You are at a facility being run by Gregor Maragos. He has hired a team specifically skilled in technology, and we have perfected nanotechnology. We have built hundreds of mosquito nanobots already. I have no idea in what manner Gregor plans to use these bots, but if it's any indication, he shot our lead scientist in the head to scare us into keeping quiet about the operation. These nanobots are capable of killing one man from thousands of miles away, or an entire army, or city, once we build enough of them. Gregor has moved his time line up again, and I fear something terrible could be about to happen. I am in the warehouse working on them now. You need to use some super spy tricks and get out of here to get word to whoever can stop this.

There will be two men coming in. You have no clock, but a door down the hall will buzz about ten seconds before they come in to give you breakfast. It is your only chance to get out of here before Gregor comes and—

Sarah stopped reading and pricked her ears. Did she just hear a buzz? Or was her mind playing tricks on her? Either way, she couldn't chance not being ready. She folded the paper and tucked it down the front of her shirt. Like a cat turning for its unknowing prey, she moved nimbly across her bed and put her back against the wall where she would be behind the door when it opened. She'd been counting down from ten from when she thought she heard the buzz.

3 . . . 2 . . . 1 . . .

The door opened. The first man inside moved toward the bed when he didn't see Sarah. As the second man was entering, Sarah front-kicked the door closed, and when the man beside the bed looked over, Sarah stepped in fast, swinging her right elbow at his head. It cracked against his right temple, and before he knew what hit him, she had already wrapped both hands around the back of his neck and pulled his head down as hard as she could, driving her knee up into his forehead. His head snapped back, and he dropped to the floor.

Sarah heard the door open behind her, and she spun in its direction, landing her right kick across the second man's midsection. He doubled over in a grunt, leaving his head exposed. Like an NFL punter, she jerked her right foot up as hard as she could and kicked him in the forehead. His head whipped back just before his body dropped.

Before she could admire her work, she felt two strong arms wrap around her upper body. The first man had been quick to recover. He squeezed and lifted her off her feet. Sarah began to pull at his exposed fingers, manipulating them backward. The man shrieked in pain and released his hold. Sarah turned and pounded his left knee with a right kick. The man buckled onto his other knee, and Sarah switched her stance, twisted her hips, and brought her left foot to his head with as much force as she could muster. Once again the man dropped unconscious. She quickly spun again, fist at the ready, but the other unconscious man wasn't as quick to recover.

She took a knee beside him, rifled through his pants until she found a set of keys. She pulled him away from the door, walked out, and locked both of them inside. She scanned the hallway. She knew more would be coming. They would have seen her handiwork on camera.

For the moment, though, she was alone.

28

Trap or Die

XANDER WATCHED as Brancati fishtailed out of the small back parking lot in a red Ford Mustang. He stood and fired in the direction of the tires, but it was no use. He turned to run for their rental car when across the street, through the smoke from the Mustang's tires, he noticed a motorcycle sitting in a driveway. It was a sport bike and, Xander figured, most likely the only way he would be able to catch up to Brancati before he disappeared.

He sprinted across the street, threw his leg over the seat, turned the key, squeezed the hand brake and the clutch, thumbed the start button, and fired up the engine. He could tell by the sound of it that it was a 1,000cc engine. Plenty of giddyup to catch Brancati. That wouldn't be the problem. It was more about what he could do from a bike once he caught up that was going to be interesting.

As he backed up then spun the bike around, Sam and Kyle came running out the back door.

"Going after Brancati!" Xander shouted.

"We'll try to catch up!" Sam shouted back.

Xander twisted the throttle with his right hand and released the clutch with his left. The motorcycle's nose rose up as it shot forward, and he rode the wheelie for about a hundred feet before the bike caught up with the acceleration and both wheels were back on the ground. Xander gave it more gas, and the crotch rocket moved forward with the speed of a bullet.

There was really only one main road in Santorini. Xander hit the brakes hard, leaned to his right, downshifted twice, and turned onto that road with his back tire sliding sideways as he once again accelerated forward.

The wind pushed back at him. He squinted through it, laid his stomach on the gas tank to become more aerodynamic, and as the road wound past the rocky caldera of Fira, the largest town on the island, he could see Brancati's Mustang in the distance. He was speeding toward Oia, the town where Xander and team stayed the night before, at the northwestern tip of the island. Last time he'd come to visit Santorini, under much more leisurely circumstances, he remembered that this road led all the way to the end of the island, dead-ending at a dock full of boats.

Brancati's exit plan.

As he sped forward, his first thought was that Brancati had been sloppy. Which did not at all correspond with his MO. Not many, if any, of Brancati's targets had ever lived through his first attempt at them. Much less a second. A thought needled at the back of his subconscious as he weaved around the slower-moving traffic: Xander was doing exactly what Brancati wanted him to do. He was quickly catching up to the Mustang. But before he could get too close, he throttled back.

This felt like a trap.

Brancati wasn't the type to smash around and make a lot of noise like back at the warehouse. But somehow, someone had clued him in that Xander would be arriving, and he had laid this trap. His hope would have been that his men could take down Xander and crew at the recycling warehouse, but leading Xander to the slaughter was almost certainly his main strategy. Xander could feel it in his bones. And he was starting to doubt this was Brancati at all in front of him. The man who had shot at him before getting into the Mustang was too far away to know for sure. Xander had just assumed it was Brancati.

Xander couldn't help but think, wherever this Mustang was leading him and whoever was driving it, that they were leading him directly to a waiting Brancati. There was no time to pull back and wait to flush him out. Xander needed to know where Sarah was, and he knew Brancati had that information. He had a feeling, too, that wherever Sarah was, he would also find Gregor Maragos—or at the very least, his weapons operation.

Xander once again leaned forward, pulled back the throttle, and gave chase. He would need to make it look like he didn't smell a trap, without tipping Brancati off and without getting killed. This was going to be a delicate balance.

Oia was just in front of them now. Xander flipped through his mind, picturing what lay ahead at the end of the road. He remembered at the top of the caldera sat a number of shops and restaurants, before the road trailed down to the boat docks. If the Mustang went all the way down to the water, Xander would be a sitting duck. There wasn't much to use for cover there. He would probably have the chance to take out the driver, but every instinct told him it wasn't Brancati.

Think.

The man driving the Mustang would have already let Brancati know that they were on the way, and that Xander was following on a motorcycle. Xander weaved around two slower cars, and he was running out of road, and time. If he were Brancati, where would he be waiting? There were a few bars and restaurants overlooking the docks, so there likely would be people having breakfast. That would make it easy for Brancati to blend in. And if Xander were Brancati, he would have the driver of the Mustang run from the car to wherever he was waiting, leading Xander right to him.

Xander needed a way to flip this around. He needed a way to make Brancati come to him. He was surprised when the Mustang came to a stop at the top of the caldera. A man got out and ran for the popular walkway along the top of the caldera—a pedestrian path that took visitors on a stroll through dozens of shops and restaurants, the height of tourism in Oia.

Xander throttled down and turned into the closest driveway he could. A hundred yards or so from where the Mustang stopped. He walked through a short alley between buildings and ducked inside a souvenir shop along the long pedestrian walkway, which was already filled with tourists. At breakfast, Xander, Sam, and Kyle had watched a cruise ship come in; Oia must have been the ship's first stop. The crowd would help Xander disappear.

Xander nodded to the shop clerk. "English?"

"Yes," the woman behind the counter said. "A little."

"Dressing room?"

The woman shook her head. "No, sorry."

Xander pulled a blue T-shirt from a rack. It had the Greek flag on it in white. Next he found a pair of board shorts, some sunglasses, and a Santorini baseball cap. He noticed a pair of white sneakers mixed in with the sandals that were for sale.

"Size thirteen?"

The clerk nodded but held up a finger. "One moment." She disappeared through an open doorway behind her.

Xander took advantage. He stripped off his clothes, changed into the tourist attire, put his extra magazine and his knife in the cargo pocket of his board shorts, and tucked his Glock in the back of his waistband just before the clerk came out with a box of sneakers. He put his things in a bag, gave her a hundred-dollar bill, grabbed a newspaper, and walked across the street to a cafe.

The man in the Mustang would have to come back for him. Xander knew Brancati wouldn't want to leave the post he'd staked out. Brancati might wait for a better opportunity, but for the best chance at not only taking down Brancati but also surviving him, this was Xander's safest and only option.

Xander ordered a coffee and took a seat at a patio table overlooking the walkway. There was no way he would miss Brancati's driver if he came back this way. With his hat pulled low, the brim touching his sunglasses, he picked up his phone to dial Sam to let her and Kyle in on his plan.

That was when he saw two missed calls and a voicemail from a Washington, DC, area code and another call he had missed just one second ago from an international number.

There was only a handful of people in the world who had his secure cell phone number. The DC number had to be the President returning his request for a call. But it was the other number that blared at him like a siren. He didn't think he would ever say it, but the President would have to wait.

He pressed the international number to call back.

A woman answered before the first ring ended. "Xander?" Her voice was a worried whisper.

"Sarah?"

29

I Just Called to Say . . .

"XANDER, I ONLY HAVE A COUPLE SECONDS," Sarah said.

After locking in the two men who had come for her, she had checked several rooms down the long hallway until she found a phone. She was huddled in the corner of an office. She could hear the two men pounding on the door down the hall. She knew more would be coming for her.

"Fill me in," Xander said.

"I was taken to Athens. In a warehouse, no other info there. Gregor Maragos's operation is here, but I haven't seen him so I'm not sure he is still here. I met an American woman named Dbie Johnson. She is the one who called for help, the one on the flash drive that one of our agents was killed for. She said Gregor has built mosquito nanobots and she is certain he's about to use them for harm. You have to find out who or what might be Gregor's target and go there immediately. I will do my best to keep Dbie safe. Don't worry about me, find Gregor and stop him before it's too late."

"I—"

A loud crash, not far from where Sarah was huddled, kept Sarah from hearing Xander's reply.

She returned the phone to her ear. "I have to go now. Stop Gregor. I'll see you soon."

She placed the phone receiver back in its cradle and walked over to the door. It was dark in the room, making it difficult for her to search for anything that could be used as a weapon. The two men who had come for her earlier weren't her concern now; she could handle them. It was the rest of the security team that had surely been called by then that worried her.

She inched the door open. Just a few feet from her in the hallway, she heard a door open, then shut. Then closer, another door opened and then shut. They were almost to her now. That was when an alarm began to sound and all of the lights turned on. Her chance of escape had just diminished considerably. The entire building was about to come down on her.

30

Cloak and Dagger

XANDER'S MOUTH dropped as Sarah hung up the phone. That was a lot of information, all of it helpful. But they were a long way from being able to stop what Xander feared was already in motion. News that Gregor had actually built workable mosquito-sized bots, effectively mastering the elusive nanotechnology, was even worse than Xander feared. The President, if Xander was right, is in worse danger than he thought. The entire world of terrorists would intensify if they didn't figure this out. This was worse than nuclear weapons. Those you could see coming, you had a chance to fight back, and it was nearly impossible to build a nuclear weapon unless you had a lot of money. With nanotechnology, even small-time terrorists could wreak global havoc from the comfort of their own home. The United States had been trying for years to get ahead of this technology. That ship had apparently sailed. This was the holy grail of modern weapons. Team Reign could not let this get away from them.

Xander forced worry about Sarah from his mind and clicked on the DC phone number to hurry and at least get some word to the President. As soon as he heard the first ring, he caught his first glimpse of the driver of the Mustang walking casually back his way. He was scanning the patios and shops for Xander. *Come on, President Williams, pick up.*

"Hello," a man finally answered.

"I'm sorry to bother you in the middle of the night, Mr. President. This is Xander King. I don't have time to explain, I just need you to get to the PEOC and stay there until we can ensure your safety."

"Xander, I . . . Emergency Operations Center? Is that really nece—"

"Get there, now. And get someone to CIA Director Mary Hartsfield's home to check on her. Also, get every government agency at your disposal doing everything they can to find a man named Gregor Maragos and any of his known associates. This is deadly serious, President Williams. Do you understand?"

Brancati's driver was just a few feet from him now. Xander needed to go. He was about to miss his window for solving at least one of his problems.

"I understand. I'll do everything you've asked."

"And do it right now."

Xander ended the call. As the driver turned his back on the walkway, Xander slipped inside the restaurant, out the side door, and into the adjacent narrow alleyway. The driver walked right by, and Xander reached out, snatched him by his black T-shirt, and pinned him with a forearm by the throat to the restaurant wall. Xander's other hand held the tip of his knife to the man's kidney. The man struggled against Xander for a moment, but finally stood still when Xander pressed his forearm against the man's Adam's apple, the blade now dipping into his skin.

"There's only one way you make it out of this alive. Grunt

once if you want to hear more. Grunt twice if you want to bleed out all over the cobblestone."

One grunt.

"Right now you're going to take out your phone, dial Brancati on speakerphone, and tell him I must have gotten spooked because I didn't follow you. Then you'll do exactly what he says. Grunt once if you understand."

Xander pressed the knife harder. The man winced. The tip had broken the skin at this point.

One grunt.

Xander removed his forearm from the man's throat and grabbed a handful of T-shirt to keep him in place. He did exactly as Xander asked and dialed Brancati.

"Where is he?" Brancati answered.

Xander had been right about the trap. Before the man answered, he pressed the blade a little more. The man winced again.

"He must have known I was leading him to you." Brancati's driver's accent was Russian. "He did not follow me. I just found his motorcycle in an alley."

Xander didn't appreciate the improv, but it wasn't bad.

"Bullshit," Brancati said. "He is watching you right now. Where are you?"

"At top of mountain. On walkway with all the restaurants and shopping. Lots of people."

"Follow the walkway all the way down to the boat. If you saw him at the warehouse, what was he wearing?"

Xander quickly mouthed what he wanted the driver to say as he pressed the knife in a little deeper. Any more pressure and it would sink the rest of the way through his skin.

"I did see him," the driver said. Then the Russian followed Xander's mouth. "He is wearing black T-shirt, black pants."

"Listen carefully," Brancati said. "He will have already called for his team. So they will be lurking as well. All I want you to do is walk to the far end of the boat dock and wait there. We will leave as soon as I have finished with King. Understood?"

Xander nodded.

"Understood," the Russian said.

Brancati ended the call.

Xander backed away from the driver, closed his knife, and pulled his pistol from his waistline. "Where is he?"

"I don't know," the driver said.

Xander pulled back the slide and released it.

The driver shook his head. "He would never tell me that. Just for this reason." The man looked Xander up and down.

Xander believed him. He pulled his phone and dialed Sam.

"Go," Sam answered.

"I have the driver of the Mustang. He was leading me into a trap. Brancati thinks I am going to follow his driver down to the docks. I've changed into tourist gear, blue T-shirt, blue-and-white board shorts, white sneakers. Where are you?"

"Already down at the docks. Good on you for sniffing out the trap."

"Any ideas?" Xander asked her.

"You say you're walking here, from the pedestrian path?"

"Yes."

"My guess is he'll be perched. Kyle and I will search possible shooting cubbyholes overlooking the docks. It's mostly cliffs on that side, so there won't be many buildings for him to be hiding in, looking over you. Does he know what you're wearing?"

"I had his driver tell him what I was wearing before I went full-blown tourist. Brancati won't see me following behind his man."

Sam said, "We'll do our best to flush Brancati out. If we're fortunate enough to find him, if he shakes loose, he will have nowhere to go but toward the docks. Let's not let him out of here."

"I talked to Sarah and the President," Xander told her.

"Busy bee," Sam said.

"Sarah's in danger in Athens. That's where they took her, and that's also where Gregor is building the weapons. He's built nanobots, Sam."

Silence on Sam's end for a moment. "Christ."

"My thoughts exactly."

"We have to head them off or something terrible is going to happen."

"My thoughts exactly," Xander repeated. "One thing at a time. While we're here, we might as well take out an assassin."

"On it."

Xander ended the call. He looked back to Brancati's driver.

"Walk. I'll be close behind." Xander looked down at his Glock. "I am pretty damn good with this thing, so don't get any ideas."

The driver nodded. Xander waved the gun, motioning the driver in the direction of the walkway.

A lot of things could go wrong. For the sake of himself, Sarah, the President, and maybe the entire free world, Xander sent up a silent prayer that starting now, for the first time since Venice, they could finally get something to go right.

31

The Best Defense Is a Good Offense

WHEN THE ALARM began to sound and all of the lights turned on, Sarah decided that the best defense was a good offense. She needed to get rid of the two men searching for her; then she desperately needed to find a weapon. She heard what she thought was the door opening to the room next door, so she slinked out into the hallway, rushed inside, and kicked the man in front of her in the back. He went flying face-first to the ground. She grabbed a laptop sitting on an adjacent desk and smashed him over the head, unconscious.

She searched the room for a weapon. Nothing. She hurried over to the filing cabinets along the wall and searched the drawers. The first three yielded nothing useful. But the fourth drawer had a roll of duct tape at the bottom. She would take what she could get.

She started the tape, pulled the unconscious man's arms and legs together, and hog-tied him. She heard a door shut just outside the room she was in. She ripped a long piece of duct tape from the roll, folded it over to stick to itself, and walked over behind the door; then, standing on a chair, she wrapped the ends of the piece of tape around each of her hands, stretching a small area of tape in between.

The second man walked through the door, and when he stopped to notice his partner subdued on the floor, Sarah jumped onto his back, wrapping her legs around his waist, and took the tape that was pulled tight between her hands and twisted it around his throat. The man first groped at his neck, but when he couldn't grab the tape, he began to claw at Sarah's arms. He whirled around the room, but Sarah just rode him like a wild stallion, pulling back on the reins as if her horse was about to run off a cliff. Finally, in desperation, the man fell onto his back. Sarah shortened the tape by wrapping it around each hand once more. She continued to pull until the man went limp.

Sarah could hear footfalls above her and muffled voices from somewhere not too far away. She kicked the man off her, checked the hallway, and ran for the door at the end of it. She looked through the small square window imbedded in the door, saw nothing, and went on through. When she shut it behind her, she saw two men walk through the door at the opposite end of the hallway she'd just come from, pistols extended. She ducked out of sight, and before her were two more hallways. The wrong decision here could mean her life. She tried to thumb through the memory of her bag-over-the-head walk yesterday, and she thought she remembered making a right turn. It wasn't much to go on, but it was all she had. She stayed low and went left. She quickly checked the three offices on the way to the end of the hallway; two were locked, and one held nothing she could use as a weapon. She made her way to the door at the end, and when she looked through this window, she was looking at a large open warehouse, full of machines, and several people manning what looked to be different stations.

This is where they were building the nanobots.

Her first instinct was to turn away from the warehouse. But when she heard a door open behind her, she pictured the two men with guns walking through, so Sarah did the only thing she could and stepped inside the warehouse. Every single eye in the place turned to look at her. She straightened her posture and decided simply to walk with confidence, like she belonged there. After a few steps, the eyes turned back to their workstations, and Sarah scanned their faces, looking for Dbie Johnson.

Her eyes finally found her at the far end of the warehouse. Dbie was staring at her, shocked. So were the two men standing on both sides of her.

The two men who were holding guns.

32

Concealed Weapon

THE SUN BEGAN to bake the island of Santorini as the morning inched closer to afternoon. The cheap T-shirt Xander was wearing felt as if the screen-printed graphic was melting into his chest. As Xander had followed the driver all the way down the steep stone walkway, the shops and restaurants had trailed off a while back, only a couple hundred feet separating them from the boat docks resting atop the calm Aegean sea. Sam had called when they were halfway down. No sign of Brancati. Hordes of people now filtered into the restaurants that overlooked the water. The eateries were situated in a half-moon, tucked into the bottom of the caldera, the walkway extending all the way to the edge of the water. On the opposite end of the half moon was the only roadway in and out.

Brancati's driver stopped for a moment in front of one of the several sea salt–worn wooden boat docks that extended fifty or so feet out over the deep blue water. Crowds of people were walking back and forth between him and Xander. Though he knew Brancati would never recognize him in his tourist attire, it was still nerve-wracking being so exposed. The Russian driver moved again, walking out onto the dock. Xander was watching him closely. He wanted to see if the driver keyed in on any one boat in particular, possibly giving away Brancati's escape boat. Though Brancati probably hadn't let him in on that little detail either.

Xander walked all the way to the dock and paused where the driver had just a moment ago. He leaned his butt against the post and pulled out his phone, dialing Sam. He never took his eye off the driver, who was now reaching the end of the dock.

"No sign of him yet, Xander," Sam answered.

"I'm at the first dock right in front of the walking path. Brancati's driver is alone at the end of the dock."

"I see you. And I see him. Kyle and I are—"

Sam suddenly went quiet. She did so because she must have seen what Xander had just witnessed at the end of the dock. One second Brancati's driver's face was staring up at the sun; the next, the top half of his head disappeared and his body fell backward into the water. Xander made no move. Made no reaction. If Brancati shot his driver from a perch overlooking the docks, he would also be able to see someone react.

"I'm assuming you saw that," Xander asked.

"I did. Was he shot?"

"Yes. High-powered rifle to be able to do that kind of damage. Silenced too, I heard no report. Had to be like you said, Brancati perched. If you are on the second level above the restaurants, he can't be far."

Sam said, "Brancati knew he wouldn't be able to find you. But he didn't want you to be able to question his driver."

Xander casually turned toward the restaurants. He gave a sweeping look at the upper level. A skilled sniper doesn't shoot with the barrel of his gun exposed. Brancati would have been situated as deep inside the room he shot from as possible and still have a good line of sight.

"Anything?" Sam asked.

"I don't see a thing."

Xander continued to scan.

"There!" Sam shouted. "At the base of the road!"

Xander looked where Sam said, but from his vantage point on the ground, he couldn't see all the way to the opposite side of the half-moon walkway. There was no way he could catch up to Brancati if he tried to make it over to the road and then run up. His only shot was to sprint the steep pedestrian walkway he'd just come down, and try to meet him at the top.

"I can't see him. What's he wearing?" Xander turned and began to run.

"White long sleeves, khaki pants, and a black duffel on his shoulder. We're stuck in the middle of the second floor, no way we can make it to him. Your only chance is to head him off once you've—"

"Run up the pedestrian walkway. I'm on my way. Get there as fast as you can."

Xander ended the call, tucked the phone in his pocket, and kicked it into high gear. Not only was the path he was running the long way up, it was far more crowded and almost impossibly steep. As he sprinted up the winding path, dodging tourists, side-stepping donkey manure from the daily trek they still made for show, and taking the steps three at a time when they came, Xander couldn't help but wonder once again who had hired Brancati. He spun to avoid taking out a lady far too old to be taking the walking path down, and after another turn in the path, he began to worry, really worry, that they hadn't been able to reach Director Hartsfield. He felt the pang of fear for her in his stomach and, along with it, a growing sense that she was somehow connected to how in the hell Brancati kept showing up everywhere Xander went. It was the only explanation.

Someone in America, someone involved with Everworld Solutions, had hired Brancati. He could feel it. And that same someone, somehow, knew Xander's every move.

It had to end right now.

33

Operation Closed

SARAH DOVE behind the closest workstation she could find as the two men beside Dbie raised their guns and began to shout at her in Greek. The rest of the people working in the warehouse cowered at their stations as the tensions rose.

Sarah was in a bad spot if you considered the men with guns pointed at her. She was in a desperately terrible spot when you considered the other two gunmen approaching behind her from the hallway. Oh, and she had no weapon.

Sarah peered over the machine in front of her at the two men flanking Dbie. Then she scanned the area around her. There were a few things—a pen, some tubing, a hanger—that would be useful as weapons in close combat yet not helpful at all long distance. But she didn't have a choice, she had to move. Two gunmen and no weapon was hard. Four gunmen and no weapon was impossible. She glanced back up and watched as Dbie took a step back from the men. They didn't notice because they were focused on Sarah. As she watched Dbie pick up a laptop on the table beside her, Sarah ran about ten feet forward and dove behind another workstation, only a few feet from the men now. The men grew more agitated and began to shout even louder; threatening to shoot. Sarah ducked behind some sort of contraption and was able to take a six-inch piece of solid metal pipe from the machine's end. She crouched into a ready stance, found Dbie's eyes, and as soon as Dbie nodded to her from behind the gunmen, Sarah sprang out over the table. Instantly, she heard the warehouse entrance door open behind her, then a man shout something in her direction—it was the two gunmen from the hallway. Dbie was screaming as she smashed the laptop over one of the gunmen's head. This distracted the second gunman near Dbie, and it was enough for Sarah to close the distance and bounce the metal bar off the second gunman's skull.

Shots rang out behind Sarah, and the workers in the room began to panic, screaming for their lives. Sarah went down with the man she had just hit over the head, took his pistol from his lifeless hand, raised up just high enough to see over the row of workstations, trained the end of the gun on the two men coming, and shot at them several times until finally both of them dropped to the ground. She looked up at Dbie who was wide-eyed and motionless.

Sarah said through labored breath, "Nice work. You saved my life."

"And you saved mine."

The man Dbie hit with the laptop stirred.

"Not yet," Sarah said. "Move over there and don't turn around until I say so." Sarah motioned toward the workstations and the onlooking workers. "All of you, turn around. You're going to hear a loud noise."

They did as Sarah asked, and Sarah put two bullets in each of the downed men's chests. Gasps came from the crowd of coworkers. Sarah couldn't afford to leave anyone alive. She didn't know how many more men they would have to go through to get out of there, but she sure as hell didn't want these guys coming back to haunt her.

"All right." Sarah addressed everyone in the warehouse. "If you know the way out, I suggest you make your way there now. This operation is officially closed."

They didn't hesitate. All of them began to make their way to the door in the back of the warehouse. Everyone except Dbie.

"Come on," Dbie said to Sarah. "I'll show you the way out. We should hurry, I've seen as many as ten men here on duty before."

Sarah dropped her empty gun and collected the one with the full magazine from the second dead gunman.

"I can't leave, Dbie. I have to find Maragos."

"He's not here," Dbie said without hesitation. "He came in about an hour ago, took the nanobot inventory, and left. I haven't seen Doctor Kruger today either, which is a first since I've been working here."

"Doctor Kruger?" Sarah said.

"Yeah, Gregor's second in command."

"Any idea where Gregor was headed?"

"No, but he was in a hurry. And he took almost every working nanobot with him."

"Almost?"

"Yeah," Dbie said. "I finished fifty more in the last hour and a half but hadn't moved them to the walk-in safe. They're right here."

Dbie walked back to her workstation. Sarah followed. Dbie moved a carbon fiber briefcase over in front of her, dialed in the lock code, and popped it open. Sarah couldn't believe her eyes. In front of her, lined in five neat rows of ten, situated on top of a bed of black foam, were fifty tiny metal mosquitos.

"And these little things can be controlled? They can be used as weapons?"

"You wouldn't believe how easy it is to maneuver them," Dbie said.

"You would never see anything like this coming. And if you did, you would never think it was anything but a little bug." Sarah was in awe.

"Exactly."

"You have a device to control these, Dbie?"

"Well . . ." She paused and looked down at her smashed laptop. "They took my phone, and the laptop was the only other method I had."

Sarah looked defeated. But ultimately the laptop didn't really matter. They just needed to get out of there and get any agency they could in Greece to find and stop Gregor Maragos.

"But . . ."

Sarah looked up with hope in her eyes. "But?"

"The controls are in the system."

"You mean Gregor was dumb enough to keep the control of these online?"

Dbie smiled. "Not exactly."

Sarah gave her a "do tell" raise of the eyebrow.

"I kind of built in a back door."

"I think I like you, Dbie Johnson."

Dbie's smile faltered a bit. "Well, before you like me too much, it's still a long shot. I would have to hack these things by their lot numbers."

"Let's walk and talk," Sarah said as she shut the briefcase. "We have to get out of here. If you are the only way we can stop these nanobots once they're deployed, I have to keep you alive."

Dbie nodded, locked the briefcase, and began walking toward the back entrance. Sarah followed, gun in hand.

"Okay, now tell me what you are trying to say, but put it in layman's terms."

"Basically I need a secure connection. Then by batches of fifty I can methodically shut them down."

They approached the door.

Sarah said, "And how many of them do they have?"

Dbie looked Sarah in the eye, and it wasn't a pleasant look. "Four thousand."

"Okay. That's a lot . . ."

Sarah cracked the door and took a look in the hallway. The hallway was clear.

Sarah continued, "And how long will it take to get control of each segment of fifty?"

Dbie's look turned from unpleasant to sorrowful. "At least thirty minutes."

Sarah's mouth dropped open.

"I have to decode each individual bot once I am logged into its own segment. It was the only back door I could build in a short amount of time."

Sarah stepped inside the hallway and motioned for Dbie to follow.

"At least you gave us a chance."

34

The Rundown

XANDER RAN off the steep part of the path and onto tourist row at the top of the caldera, dodging people as they walked in and out of shops and restaurants. Sweat was pouring off him. His shirt was soaked through, his heart was pounding, and he was running out of gas. He looked to his left, where there were alleyways in between the buildings, but he saw no sign of Brancati. Just cars passing by on the roadway that Brancati had started up a couple minutes prior. The same road he could have already escaped on if he'd stolen a car.

Xander dodged people long enough to make it to where he had ditched the motorcycle earlier, but before getting on, he ran to the road to have a look. First he looked in the direction of the sea, toward the bottom of the caldera. Nothing suspicious. Then he looked right, toward the interior of the island, and along the long curve of the road, he could faintly see a car swerve around another before it sped away.

Brancati.

Xander whipped out his phone and ran for the motorcycle. In the direction Brancati was going, there were only two ways off the island: the airport and the marina at the opposite end. Knowing whether or not Brancati was going for the airport would be easy.

"This is Bob," Xander's pilot, a former Air Force captain, answered the phone.

"Bob, this is important. Our man is coming your way. All I need you to do is let me know if he makes it to the airport. Only call me if he makes it to the airport."

"You got it. Anything else?"

Xander ended the call, picked up the motorcycle, and dialed Sam.

"Yes, Xander?"

"Get a boat and take it to the marina on the opposite side of the island. I'll meet you there. Be ready for a fight."

"Done."

Xander put his phone away and fired up the motorcycle. A few seconds later he was doing 130 miles an hour, desperately trying to make it to Brancati before he once again slipped away.

———

XANDER LEANED into the right turn and sped his way toward Blycháda, the marina at the southern tip of Santorini. The call from Bob never came, so this was the only place Brancati could be. As Xander sped down the caldera, he scanned the marina below him. There were three arching concrete slips that boats were tied off to, then a rock barrier along the outside to protect the boats from wake, then the Aegean Sea. As he looked for movement, for a man Brancati's size running for a boat, he noticed a small boat speeding toward the marina from the sea.

It was Sam and Kyle.

He didn't see any other boats. For the moment, it seemed as though he wasn't too late. There would be no time for subtlety; he wouldn't be trying to sneak up on Brancati. Quite the opposite. He would smash his way through this marina if need be. He was a minute or so behind Brancati, and that might be long enough to lose him, so time was of the essence.

Xander zoomed down the rest of the winding road, skidded to a halt, let the bike fall on its side, pulled his Glock, and ran for the boat slips. The marina was bustling. Fishermen coming in and out, tourists leaving and returning from boat excursions, and now an American agent trying to run down an assassin before he got away and regrouped to try to murder said American agent again.

Xander ran past the small marina office, and in the middle of the concrete boat slip that arched out into the water, Brancati was running toward a boat.

"Everyone, get inside the office and get down on the ground!" Xander shouted at the crowd of people gathered in front of the office. He put a period on his command by firing two shots into the air. Behind him he heard shouts of fear, but there was no time to see if they were complying. For the first time, Xander locked eyes with Brancati as he turned from the middle of the boat slip, presumably to see where the gunshots had come from. Xander plodded to a stop and steadied his gun in front of him. When he squeezed the trigger twice, Brancati dove into the fishing boat to his right. Xander took two steps before he had to stop again. Rounding the concrete boat slip from behind Brancati were two men, and they were firing as they ran.

Xander dove to the ground and rolled behind a large metal equipment bin where fisherman stored their gear. A couple bullets skipped off the concrete, and a couple more pounded against the other side of the bin.

Though Xander was pinned, he felt as fortunate as he had since this entire operation started. As soon as Sam and Kyle tied off their boat, it would be three on three. A fight in Xander's favor. Brancati may be good, but his men weren't as good as Sam and Kyle. Xander would take that to the bank.

His phone began to vibrate.

"Sam, I'm on the boat slip."

"Good. I just saw two men running your way. I assumed they were shooting at you. Any sign of Brancati?"

"Just dove into a boat. But not his. Tie off and come up behind them. I'll keep them from getting out this way."

"Copy."

Xander put his phone away and peeked over the top of the bin. A few more shots came his way. He ducked back down. The men were trapped between him and Sam, but this was going to get ugly.

"Xander!" Brancati shouted.

He was ready to negotiate. He must have seen Sam and Kyle coming up behind him.

"Xander, we can work this out. No need for you to die here today."

Xander answered by shooting a couple bullets in the direction of the boat. A few more shots returned back at him.

"Stop shooting!" Brancati shouted. "I know where your agent is. I will tell you and we both can leave here."

Xander shouted from a crouch behind the bin. "I know where Sarah is too. And you're right, we both *will* leave here. Me on my plane and you in a body bag."

Xander heard Sam and Kyle's boat motor shut down at the other end of the slip.

"All right," Brancati shouted. "You already know where your agent is. Fine. I have something more important anyway. Something I am sure you have been wondering about . . ."

Xander didn't respond.

Brancati finished. "Who hired me."

35

Embassy Sweets

SARAH AND DBIE had come to their second exit door as they tried to escape the warehouse. The first door they tried, they found two men holding guns on the workers who had tried to leave. They were frisking them and most likely asking if they had seen Sarah. Sarah was now peeking out of a door that overlooked a parking lot. There were several cars and no sign of any people. More importantly, no sign of anyone holding a gun.

"We're going to make a run for it," Sarah told Dbie. "When we reach the cars, just start checking to see if any of them are open and if any of them have keys."

"You can't hot-wire one?"

"Unfortunately, they didn't teach me grand theft auto in training."

Dbie frowned. Sarah pushed open the door and ran for the cars.

"Just yell at me when you find one with keys and get in the passenger seat!"

Dbie didn't answer, and they both began tugging on door handles as quickly as they could. After Sarah found her third locked car in a row, she glanced back at the warehouse and saw the door they'd just exited swing open.

"Get down, Dbie!"

It was all she had time to shout. As the two men raised their guns, Sarah raised hers. They managed to get their shots off first, a string of bullets in Dbie's direction. Sarah wasn't sure if Dbie had been able to take cover in time. She returned fire, missing with her first couple shots, then connecting with the man on the left with her next two. The gunman beside him dove behind a car to regroup.

"Dbie, are you okay?" Sarah shouted as she continued pulling on car door handles. "Dbie!"

"I found one," Dbie's muffled voice came back. "It has keys!"

Sarah moved toward her voice. She fired two rounds in the direction of the gunman. She saw a black Toyota Avalon with the door askew. She rushed toward it and jumped in the driver's seat. Dbie was slinked as low as she could be on the passenger side.

"Nice find!" Sarah told her as she started the car.

The gunman rose from behind the sedan where he was taking cover. Sarah slammed the car in reverse, and tires screamed against the pavement as she drove the car backward.

"Stay down!" she told Dbie as the man, now only about twenty feet away, began to fire.

The passenger window shattered inward, and Dbie screamed. Sarah turned the wheel to the left and stomped on the gas pedal. The Avalon shot backward, and as the man began to fire again, shattering the back window, Sarah turned the wheel once more and the car spun 180 degrees. Sarah flinched hard, then ducked her head on instinct, and the Avalon sideswiped the last three cars in the lot. But the car was okay and Sarah sped away. In the distance, she saw a gated entrance with a guard house in front of the closed exit.

Sarah glanced over at Dbie when she saw her right hand move at her side.

"Are you all right?"

Dbie didn't need to answer with words. The blood on her hand spoke for itself.

"Damn it, Dbie! How bad is it?"

The Avalon was flying toward the guard house. A man in a security uniform stepped out of the door and in front of the striped boom barrier that was lowered to keep people from leaving. Sarah looked back to Dbie.

"How bad?" Sarah shouted.

"I-I don't know. I don't know!" Dbie was scared.

Sarah couldn't help her unless she got her out of there, so she turned her attention back to the man she was rocketing toward.

"What are you doing? Slow down!" Dbie shouted.

But she couldn't slow down. Two SUVs had pulled out behind her. It was clear that Maragos's men had orders to kill. Sarah slammed the gas pedal, aiming the center of the car's hood right at the gate guard who began to raise his gun. Just before she slammed into him, he dove out of the way. The car busted through the wooden boom barrier, then crashed through the chain link fence surrounding the property. Sarah stomped on the brake, wheeled hard to the right, and the back end of the car skidded across the pavement, dragging some of the ruined fence beneath it.

Sarah slowed enough for the tires to regain purchase, and when she looked back over her shoulder, the two SUVs were already turning onto the road behind her.

"Can you work the GPS?" Sarah asked Dbie. "Neither of us have a phone and we have to get to the American embassy, right now. It's our only chance."

Dbie sat up in her seat, leaned forward, and starting

punching away at the GPS in the car's dashboard. "Yeah, I can do it."

Sarah swerved around two cars and took a quick left turn. Cars skidded to a stop and laid on their horns. The SUVs followed right behind her. There was no way she was going to be able to lose them.

"The embassy?" Sarah said in a panic.

"I'm trying!"

As the SUVs were coming right up to her bumper, she jerked the steering wheel right and cut off a car, skidding against their front end but making the turn and putting a little distance between them and Maragos's men. It didn't last. The SUVs were bigger and faster, and they were about to—

One of the SUVs slammed into the Avalon's back bumper, surging them forward. Sarah swerved around the car in front of her, then swerved farther left up onto a sidewalk just to avoid an oncoming car, crashed through a table of produce, then swerved back right and into the proper lane.

"Dbie!"

"Got it!"

The GPS, the only calm voice in the car, told them to turn right in two-tenths of a mile.

Sarah swerved left, then followed the GPS directions, almost going onto two wheels as she made the right turn.

The GPS chimed in again, "In one mile, your destination is ahead on the left."

SLAM!

The SUV once again crashed into their back bumper. This time Sarah momentarily lost control. When the car veered right, she turned it back left, but the back end slid out on her. She pressed the accelerator once again and wheeled back to the right. This straightened her up, and the SUV slamming into her again jerked the car forward. As she sped away, the second SUV came up beside her on her right. Sarah was no stranger to driving a car, but she had never been in any kind of situation like this. In the back of her mind, however, she heard Xander's voice, remembering somehow the time he had told her that the best defense is a good offense. She sure hoped that was true.

Before the SUV could try to sideswipe her, Sarah jerked the wheel to the right, and their little Avalon plowed into the side of the SUV. It didn't move it much, but it did force the driver to apply the brakes to avoid hitting a parked car on the right side of the road.

"There!" Dbie shouted. "There's the American flag! It's the embassy!"

Old glory had never looked so beautiful waving in the hot afternoon Athenian sun. Just as Sarah hit the gas pedal again, she heard a crunch at the back of their car, and it began to spin out of control. The momentum of the car carried the spin forward and into the three lanes of oncoming traffic. The large square embassy was just in front of them now. But cars were careening around them, desperately trying to avoid a crash.

The car continued to spin. "When the car stops, jump out and run for the embassy," Sarah shouted. "I'll cover you! Tell them I am CIA Special Agent Sarah Gilbright!"

Two more full revolutions later, the car came to a stop, and so did the two SUVs. Sarah was facing them as four men got out of the two vehicles.

Sarah pulled her pistol and shot right through the windshield at them. "Go! Go! GO!" she screamed to Dbie.

The men ducked for cover, and Dbie slid out the passenger door, sprinting for the embassy. Sarah opened her door with her left hand as she continued squeezing the trigger with her right. She eased her way out of the car, squeezing three more times before she reached the trunk; then her trigger clicked, the slide locked, her magazine was empty. She crouched behind the back of the beaten-up Avalon. When she peeked over the trunk, she expected to see guns pointed at her. Instead, with great relief, she saw the men getting back in their trucks.

Sarah looked over her shoulder and saw two uniformed men running her way. It was then that she realized just how hard she was breathing, her hands shaking from the adrenaline rush. She made it. *They* made it. The embassy guards helped her to her feet and began walking her to safety. In front of her, people were frantically moving about in front of the embassy, and she realized that sirens were sounding.

"Is this because of me?" Sarah asked the guards.

"That depends, ma'am, did you have anything to do with the terrorist attack?"

36

Silence, Assassin

WHEN BRANCATI SHOUTED, "WHO HIRED ME?" Xander had to take a moment. It was a good tactic. Brancati had to know that Xander would want this information over all other things. The problem was, whoever Brancati claimed had sent him, Xander wouldn't be able to trust his word. Sure, he could take the time to figure out if what Brancati was saying was true, but he wouldn't know that in the here and now. So what good would it do? It could only serve to get him killed. And that wasn't on the afternoon's agenda.

"Okay, Brancati," Xander said, playing along. "Who hired you?"

Xander tucked his pistol in his board shorts, dropped onto his stomach, slid over to the edge of the dock, and lowered himself into the water. He held onto the concrete slip with both hands, keeping his chest and head above the water.

Brancati shouted back. "And what do I get in return for this information?"

"Let me think about that," Xander shouted back.

He immediately began to shimmy along the edge of the dock in the direction of Brancati and his men. They were on the opposite side of the concrete slip, about four boats down. Xander passed under the rope of the first tied-off fishing boat.

"How about a million dollars? Who doesn't like money, am I right?"

Obviously Xander couldn't answer, it would give away his new position. Instead, he doubled the speed of his hand-over-hand shimmy down the boat slip. He made his way under the rope tied to the second boat and was almost to the third.

"Xander, now is not the time to go quiet . . . Xander!"

Xander let go with his right hand, pulled his pistol, lifted himself up to where his head was above the boat slip, hooked his left elbow on the concrete, and held his gun steady, locked on the side of the boat that Brancati was negotiating from. He could only see the shoulder of Brancati in his sights, but one of his men stuck out like a sore thumb. Better to take one down completely than merely injure Brancati.

Xander squeezed the trigger twice, and the large man in the blue polo shirt took two in the chest, dropping to the deck of the boat. Brancati moved behind the bulkhead of the fishing boat while his other gunman swung his gun in Xander's direction. Xander's elbow slipped as he fired, and his bullets went awry. He heard two shots from the gunman's direction, then four shots from farther away. By the time Xander pulled himself back up, the gunman was gone, and out of the corner of his eye he noticed Sam and Kyle, both on one knee, their guns trained on Brancati's fishing boat.

Then he heard a splash.

"He's making a swim for it," Kyle shouted.

Xander pulled himself up on the boat slip and saw Brancati making a swim for shore. The way the beach was arched behind the boat slips, swimming was definitely the most direct route. If

Xander didn't move now, there was a chance Brancati could get to the parking lot before he could run around the slip and meet him there. So he broke into a sprint, digging deep, blasting forward with powerful strides. He heard gunshots behind him, then saw splashes around Brancati in the water. Sam and Kyle were shooting at him, but they were too far away to get a good shot. So was Xander at this point. If he stopped to shoot, and missed, Brancati would be a ghost.

Xander rounded the boat slip onto the pavement that ran alongside the marina office. Brancati was running ashore, about fifty yards away. Xander jumped the rope separating the beach from the pavement as Brancati ran up the hill toward the beach parking lot. There were several beachgoers cowering and running for cover, so stopping to shoot here wasn't an option, and the same went for Sam and Kyle. Xander was going to have to run him down.

The sand gave beneath each step, sucking his feet into the earth as if he was in quicksand. Brancati was reaching the pavement of the parking lot, so he began to put distance between them. Xander trudged through several more soft steps, then easier ones as the sand hardened, then finally he too was up the hill and in the parking lot. And that's where he stopped. There was no sign of Brancati. Obviously he was hiding behind one of the vehicles, but there were more than fifty there on this hot sunny day. He crouched for more cover behind the first row of cars as he scanned the parking lot. He glanced behind him and saw Sam and Kyle running on the beach. He motioned for them to make their way around the right side of the parking lot to get a better angle.

"This is over, Brancati," Xander shouted, still crouched behind a car, pistol extended. His breathing was returning to normal after the sprint. "Give it up. No way out of here."

As Brancati sprinted from one row of cars to the next, Xander squeezed the trigger twice, missing, and the second squeeze locked the slide. He was out of bullets. Brancati rose from his crouch and fired twice at him. Xander ducked down, the bullets clanking into the car in front of him. Sam and Kyle opened fire from Xander's right. When Xander saw Brancati turn his attention to them, he sprinted around to the left, moving up behind Brancati. Sam and Kyle fired several more times, Brancati returned fire, and as Xander turned his sprint down the row of cars Brancati was shooting from, he watched as Brancati shot his last bullet, turned to run, and was now coming right at Xander with a shocked look on his face.

Xander lowered his head and tackled Brancati at the waist like a linebacker stopping a running back from reaching the goal line. The force of the hit knocked most of the air from Brancati's lungs, and Xander landing on top of him took the rest. Xander quickly passed Brancati's guard and moved into full mount position. He postured up, lifting his fist to strike, but Brancati was ready. He bucked his hips and threw Xander off balance. When Xander moved to regain balance, Brancati shrimped out, pushing away from Xander, and bounced to his feet, throwing a kick at Xander's head almost before Xander could move. But Xander did manage to get his head out of the way, and Brancati's leg struck hard against his shoulder instead.

Xander staggered backward from the force, and he instantly felt a jab and a right cross to the right side of his face. Brancati was fast. He didn't hit hard, but he was like lightning. Two more punches came, but Brancati threw them too hard and put himself off balance. After dodging the punches, Xander moved in; he would use his weight and strength to gain the advantage. He wrapped his hands around the back of Brancati's neck, and as he pulled his head down, he brought his knee up to meet his forehead. A solid connection.

Xander took advantage of Brancati's dazed state and once again took the fight to the ground, putting Brancati on his back and moving straight to a mount. He brought his fist up behind his ear and brought an elbow down on Brancati's head like an anvil. Brancati instantly went unconscious. The back of his head pounded into the pavement. Xander reached back wanting to give him one more for Jack and Zhanna, but as he brought his elbow down, he felt someone yank him back, tearing him away from Brancati.

Xander jerked away, turned with his hands up ready for a fight, but all he saw was his friend Kyle.

"X! Calm down! You can't kill him. We need information!"

Xander was a raging bull. He turned back, looking down over Brancati, his chest heaving, his lip bleeding, his adrenaline rushing. He wanted more. He wanted Brancati to feel more pain for killing an American agent. For having his friends shot and for putting Sarah in danger.

Sam stepped in. "Xander, calm down. You've done it. You got him. Now we can move on to more important things."

Sam put her hand on Xander's shoulder, but Xander quickly tore himself away and walked to the edge of the parking lot. The beach below him was still littered with frightened patrons. The water beyond them rolled gently along, a calm day for the sea. He took a couple slow deep breaths. The water in front of him was serving well to quench the fire that was burning inside of him. A couple more deep breaths. Once again, Sam was right. He wanted Brancati to die. To pay the ultimate price. But what mattered was that he would no longer be able to distract Xander and his team from what was really important: the global threat that confronted them.

"It's all right now," he called down to the people on the beach. "It's over. The police will be here shortly to question you."

He turned back toward Sam and Kyle, his focus returning to where it needed to be. On Gregor Maragos and his army of little death machines.

37

Under Attack

XANDER, Sam, and Kyle followed Bob up the stairs and boarded the jet. Xander took a few minutes to wash up and change out of his Santorini's finest tourist wear. They were soaked through with sweat and spotted with blood. He cleaned up the small cut on his lip as well. Santorini hadn't gone exactly the way they wanted it to, but so far with this mission, what had? They weren't completely able to solve this thing on their own, but they did get valuable information from the reporter about how Gregor's father's death went down. Xander felt they had some good leads on who was helping Gregor fund and hide his operation. If they could find who did him wrong within the Everworld corporation, that just might lead them to the culprit. Problem was, now that Sarah had hard info on the weapons Gregor had built, that was all they had time to focus on: stopping them. Finding everyone responsible would have to come later.

As Xander walked out of the bathroom and took a seat opposite Sam and Kyle, he was grateful that he no longer had an assassin breathing down his neck. They couldn't get Brancati to talk. No surprise. They left him in the custody of the Santorini police. Not Xander's first choice, but they had no time to babysit him on the plane. Two American agents were on their way to apply some needed *pressure*, but Xander knew Brancati wouldn't talk. At the very least, now Xander had a little more room to breathe and focus on the task at hand. You know, saving the free world. Speaking of saving, Xander was unable to save his phone. When he dipped down into the sea at the boat slip, it had taken in too much water. It was completely fried.

"I feel naked without my phone," Xander told his two friends. "Especially with all that's going on. I have Sarah who could be calling, the director of the CIA hopefully trying to find me, and oh, no big deal, the President of the United States."

"Aren't you Mister Popularity," Sam said.

"Was that a joke? From Sam?" Xander finally let himself laugh.

"She didn't mean to," Kyle said. "All her jokes are accidents."

"Anyway . . ." Sam pulled on the reins. "All of those people have my number if they need to talk to you. You need to catch us up, Xander. We need to know where to go from here."

Xander started by letting them know that he told the President to go into lockdown until he heard from Xander himself. Then he explained the situation that Sarah was in. She no longer had her phone either, and they didn't know if she made it out of Maragos's warehouse alive.

Kyle said, "So we're headed for Athens?"

Xander was getting ready to say yes and then ask if Sam had heard from Director Hartsfield, when Bob came storming into the cabin from the cockpit.

"You might want to turn on the news. I'm not sure what's going on, but I have a feeling you're going to want to see this."

Xander's stomach dropped. Had the President not made it to

the Emergency Operations Center? Was Director Hartsfield dead?

When Sam hit power on the remote, both flat screen televisions fixed to the back wall of the jet powered on. A helicopter view hovering over the Acropolis in Athens displayed the scene, and a graphic at the bottom explained that twenty-five American students were battling for their lives at a local hospital, five others dead.

"Turn it up," Xander said.

Images of the Acropolis, ambulances, and teenage kids on stretchers moved across the screen as the reporter told the story:

You are looking at images from earlier this morning at the Acropolis in Athens, Greece, where a group of American students were here to see the sites as a part of their History Club trip. Witnesses reported seeing them begin to panic and run around like they had walked through a hornet's nest, swatting at the air, shouting. Very quickly they began to fall ill, so much so they couldn't get themselves down from the Acropolis. What was found at the scene by police is going to sound like I am telling you about a science fiction movie, but unfortunately this unbelievable story is real. Before the police were able to clear the scene, one witness was able to snap a photo of what the teens were running from.

The image on the screen changed to a closeup of a hand, palm up, holding what looked like a mosquito. Then the camera zoomed in on the mosquito, and it was clearly a nanobot. Just like Sarah had described to Xander in the few seconds they spoke on the phone.

"Maragos," Xander said.

What you are looking at is some sort of tiny robot. Like a mini drone. That is all the information we have at this time. The police were quick to take the object into custody, and haven't said a word about it since. As for the teens, whatever these robots are, and whoever was controlling them, apparently injected the teens with some sort of poison, or virus. At this point it is still unclear. What is clear is that we have a new and absolutely terrifying threat, and there are a couple dozen teens fighting for their lives because of it. One can only think of some sort of technologically advanced terrorist being behind this. And right now, we can only hope this is the end of it. I'll have more for you when someone in law enforcement decides to give us more information.

Xander, Kyle, and Sam all gave each other a worried look.

"Are we too late?" Kyle asked.

Xander was quiet. While Kyle's first thought was about the past, Xander's was about the future.

"How do we get ahead of this, Sam? We are the people they call when something like this is going down. We've got to know where to point our plane."

"We first have to find out where Gregor is. Marvin is at headquarters combing every flight in and out of Athens. If Gregor left the country, his team will find him."

"And if he hasn't left?" Kyle asked.

"Then Greece's National Intelligence Service will have to find him," Xander answered. "And we have to make sure that whoever is helping Gregor doesn't manage to get these things into America."

"You think it's an American helping him, don't you?" Sam asked.

"I'm sure of it. And I'm afraid their mutual vendetta is against our President."

Sam's phone began to ring. She looked up at Xander, her face indicating that she didn't recognize the number.

"It's Sarah," Xander said.

Sam hit the speaker button and handed him the phone.

"Are you all right?" he asked her when he answered.

"Xander, there's been an attack on Americans, it was Maragos. He was testing the nanobots."

"I know, we just saw it on the news."

"I've been in contact with Marv. Xander, I tried to call

Director Hartsfield but I couldn't reach her. I can always reach her."

"I know that too. We have people headed to check on her. What did Marv say?"

"I told him to get a team over to the warehouse and lock it down. And he said he already has a team hunting Gregor Maragos. We can't let Maragos leave Greece. This attack here was on Americans, and I don't believe that was a coincidence."

"We agree," Xander said. "Good call on the warehouse. If you and Marv have things under control in Athens, we are going to head straight back to the States to try to get ahead of this thing if it is coming to American soil."

"You can't." Sarah was blunt. "You have to come here. I have the only person in the free world with me who can control these things for the good guys."

"What do you mean?"

"I have Dbie Johnson. She's the one who made the call. The call that got our agent killed, but she's the one in position to fight this before it gets worse. She built in a back door to these nanobots' software, Xander. She's given us a chance to control them."

"Where is she?"

"She's working away at a computer now. She took a bullet to the leg on our way out of the warehouse, but she's been patched up and is committed to getting control of these things. It takes time to hack in. Do you have the capabilities on the jet to allow her to keep hacking as we fly to the US?"

"I don't know, what does she need?" Xander asked.

"Apparently just an internet connection. She's savvy as hell."

"Well yeah, we've got that. I have a satellite that'll keep us up and running even over the ocean."

"Marvin told me you had the President go into lockdown. You think he's in danger?"

"I know he is."

"Then we have to get the hell back home."

Xander couldn't agree more. "Get to the airport, we'll be there in forty minutes."

Bob heard the conversation and was already back in the cockpit firing up the engines.

"We have to find Maragos, Xander." Sarah's tone was dire.

"Marv will find him. Son of a bitch could spot a birthmark on a fly's ass from three thousand miles away."

"You'd better pray you're right. Gregor has hundreds more of these things. And as the American teenagers dying over at the hospital shows, he's not afraid to use them."

38

A Lot Out of a Little

THE TIRES on the landing gear screeched against the runway as Xander and crew touched down in Athens. A forty-minute flight wasn't a long time, but they had managed a lot on the short trip. Ten minutes was lost trying to explain to Kyle exactly what nanotechnology was. Xander was very familiar. Nanotechnology itself was nothing new. They had been making use of it in the military for a while. It could be found in many things, like the bulletproof vest. But nanotechnology in the capacity that Gregor Maragos had managed was something new entirely. And something that could completely change the future of combat. If you could send one mosquito bot into a meeting room to gather information or send it under the door in a hostage negotiation, it could save lives on a large scale. Not to mention the recon these tiny things could do on a SEAL mission. Xander would have killed to have this technology when they were going in blind into enemy territory. It would have changed everything.

Kyle was in awe, but it was when Xander explained why the President was in so much danger that the scope of this mission really sank in. One nanobot sent in from thousands of miles away could take out the President and change the course of American politics in an instant. It was the biggest breakthrough since the nuclear weapon and, as Sam stated to Kyle, even more dangerous in scope. Nuclear weapons are far easier to track and regulate. These silent little killers are cheap, and they can go unnoticed. A thousand of them could wipe out an army in seconds.

After catching Kyle up to speed, they finally heard from Director Hartsfield. She was alive. Two CIA agents had to bust into her home to wake her, but she was fine. She chalked it up to too much wine, but Xander knew Mary pretty well. When something this big was going down, she was always on top of her game. He didn't have time to delve further; they all had to focus on Maragos. If they could stop him here in Athens, they could lock this thing down and contain it to this one attack. Marv had been tracking every airport, boat dock, flight, and any other location that Maragos could use for an exit. Not only Gregor but also his brother, Andonios, and because Dbie provided her name, they were also tracking Gregor's second in command, Doctor Emilia Kruger. There had been no sign of Doctor Kruger; her name hadn't appeared in any ticketing capacity as leaving Athens. But luckily for them, Xander had been right about Marvin's skills: the facial recognition software had shown a hit on Gregor himself.

The jet taxied to the private terminal away from the fray at Athens International Airport.

"I don't want anyone to make a move until we get there," Xander said.

Marvin had tracked Gregor Maragos to a street camera just outside of an office building downtown. The local paparazzi had taken pictures of him and Andonios at a cafe down the street from this same building on several occasions. Marv figured this meant they had spent time in the area for business, and he had put facial recognition software to use on all of the street cameras within a few blocks of the cafe just in case there was a spot Gregor might use to hide out. A few hours ago, he had walked into the building, and as far as Marv could tell from the fifteen cameras in the immediate area, he had yet to leave.

Sam said, "Marv's team has been told to stand down. They have the building inconspicuously surrounded. But something feels off to me, Xander."

He nodded. "I feel the same way. Makes no sense that he would so publicly enter a building and just stay there. He is smarter than that. My guess is we've missed him leaving somehow."

"I hope you're wrong, but I think you're right."

"Make sure Marv keeps checking the flights out of here," Xander said.

"We have Greek agents everywhere, at every terminal. Including this private one."

The door of the jet opened, and the stairs unfolded to the tarmac below. When Xander stepped out, the heat rushed in, but he didn't feel it. His senses were all focused on the blonde hurrying toward the plane. Other than the brief moment Xander saw Sarah at the museum in Venice, the last time he saw her was when they decided it was best to part ways. One of the hardest conversations he'd ever had, yet it had been made easy by this brilliant, beautiful woman, who was now smiling ear to ear in front of him, her arms stretched wide. Xander descended the stairs and took her in his arms.

He said, "I'm so glad you're okay."

As always, she smelled of lavender and honey. An intoxicating mix that had always melted Xander's tough exterior. She stepped back and looked him over.

"I'm lucky. And from the looks of it, so are you," Sarah said.

Xander smiled. "Luck never has anything to do with it."

"Xander, this is Dbie."

He hadn't even noticed another person standing there.

"I hear you are the star of the show."

"I'm just happy to be out of the madhouse," Dbie replied.

"You two can stay on the plane while we go check on Maragos."

Sarah scoffed. "Not a chance. This is personal."

Xander nodded, then turned to his friend. "Kyle, you mind staying back with Dbie and making sure she's safe while we run this thing down."

"Not at all."

Xander said to Dbie, "How far have you gotten?"

"About two hundred bots taken offline. So, a long way to go."

Sam interrupted, "Xander, we have to go. Dbie, you'll find every comfort you need aboard the plane. Thank you for your help."

Sam walked away.

"Thank you for getting me out of here," Dbie said to Xander. "Sarah saved my life."

Xander looked into Sarah's blue eyes. "Yeah, she's pretty damn good at that."

Kyle ushered Dbie onto the plane, and Sarah and Xander caught up with Sam. The three of them rode together with some agents from Greek intelligence toward the downtown district. All of them hoping they could nip this monumentally dangerous situation in the bud before it got any worse.

39

Through the Fog

CIA DIRECTOR MARY HARTSFIELD shut the door to her office.

"What the hell happened last night, Graham?"

The entire morning since she'd been woken by two of her agents had been a fog. She tried to piece together the evening but couldn't remember a thing past that gin martini at Graham's.

"I didn't think I had *that* much to drink. How did I even get home?"

She heard Graham laugh through the phone. "My martinis are notoriously strong, and you were sucking them down fast. You really don't remember me taking you home?"

She paused, once again trying to conjure the memory from blackness.

"I really don't."

"I'm really sorry. I know you have a lot going on, I didn't mean to get you drunk."

"No, it's my fault," she said with a sigh. "I guess the weight of what is going on was good to escape from and I got a little carried away. Thank you for taking care of me."

"Don't mention it. Everything okay at work today?"

"It's fine, but I best get going."

"When can I see you again, Mary?"

"Soon. Let me get through the madness here and I'll call you, okay?"

"Sounds good. Keep us safe, would you?"

Mary smiled. "I'll do my best. Thanks again, Graham."

Mary ended the call and walked out of her office. She was genuinely furious with herself. She put her entire team in danger by not being able to respond to them. Something she didn't take lightly. She had put in far too many years to get to this position. She certainly wasn't going to make it here and then risk the lives of men and women laying it all on the line for their country.

She walked down the hall and entered the meeting room that she had deemed mission control for the Maragos situation. Marvin noticed her and immediately walked away from his agent working at her computer. The midthirties man looked much older than he was. His hair already gray. His fashion like an AARP ad. But none of that mattered here. His brilliant mind was all the CIA and Mary Hartsfield cared about.

Marvin pushed his black-rimmed glasses up the bridge of his nose. "Good to see that you are okay. The team was worried about you."

Mary was embarrassed, but she didn't let on. "Show me the latest."

Marv nodded and walked over to three monitors.

"These are three different angles of the building Maragos entered a few hours ago."

"No sign he's come out?" Mary asked.

"No. People have come and gone, but our software hasn't found any matches to Gregor himself."

"What about this Doctor Kruger?"

"No Emilia Kruger has bought a plane ticket, rented a car, or purchased a boat ride."

"What about your facial recognition software?"

Marvin looked disappointed. "We've yet to find a photo. We got a late start on her. Until Sarah got the information about her from the American woman working at Maragos's site, we didn't know she existed. I have two researchers looking into her background now."

"Okay, anything else?"

"Team Reign has just pulled up to the building. Xander, Sam, and Sarah Gilbright are going in in just a moment."

"Oh good, Sarah is with them too." Mary was glad to hear she was okay and ready to jump back in. Sarah was a top-notch agent, a good woman to have in a pinch.

Marvin said, "As for the recycling company in Santorini, and the Everworld corporation that Xander told us to look into, it's all a bit murky. But I'm personally combing through it. Something is definitely amiss. Someone good at hiding things and moving money on the down low has had their hands in at least the recycling company but maybe Everworld as well."

"President Williams isn't going to like this. I'll call him and see if he can offer any suggestions on where we should look."

"Oh good." Marvin was relieved. "We need some insider info, but obviously I have no line of communication with the President."

"I'll call—"

Marvin interrupted, "Oh look, Xander is going in now."

"I'll call the President after I see what happens here. Maybe I can get the info you need, as well as deliver some good news to the President about Gregor Maragos."

40

Hold That Elevator

XANDER APPROACHED the entrance to the building. He, Sam, and Sarah had changed into business attire. Greek intelligence officers had loaned them briefcases to match their suits. They entered the seven-story office building that they were told housed customer service reps for several local businesses. Nothing out of the ordinary. One floor was for an insurance company. The owner's name was Henry Panos. Upon deeper investigation, Marvin had found there was no activity for a Henry Panos on any credit cards, bank statements, or any other form of documentation. Henry Panos was a shell. Xander approached the welcome desk.

"I'm here for a meeting with Mr. Panos."

"Of course, just a moment," the young woman said.

She tapped around on a keyboard as she scanned a computer screen.

"I don't see that Mr. Panos has any meetings scheduled today. But this isn't uncommon. Let me call up to his receptionist—"

"Actually, it's kind of a surprise. He's an old university friend of mine and I wanted to pop in on him."

The dark-haired woman smiled. "I'm sorry. I can't let you up without notifying him first. It's strict policy."

Xander let his face sadden.

"I had a whole thing planned to surprise him. He always gets me and . . ." Xander looked over his shoulder at Sam and Sarah, giving them a wink. He nodded toward Sam, then pulled his best puppy dog eyes for the receptionist. "Can you keep a secret, Miss . . ."

He paused for her name.

"Iliana."

"Iliana." Xander smiled. "Beautiful name. Can you keep a secret, Iliana?"

"I suppose." She played along.

He nodded to Sam again. "This is Iris, Henry's sister. He hasn't seen her in a long time and has no idea she's in town. I'd really love to surprise him with this."

Xander gave Iliana a moment. She tucked a loose strand of hair behind her ear and gave a wry smile. "That's really sweet. I guess I can make an exception, but if he asks, you snuck by, okay? No offense, but he's pretty scary."

Xander smiled. "You keep my secret, I'll keep yours."

She smiled and nodded. "Fourth floor. Make a right off the elevator and go all the way to the end of the hall."

"You're a lifesaver."

Xander gave her a wink, and the three of them walked around the corner to the elevator.

"Iris?" Sam said.

Xander scoffed. "I charm the receptionist into letting us pass unnoticed, and all you're worried about is what name I gave you?"

The three of them got into the elevator. Sarah laughed at the two of them.

"Good to see the two of you haven't changed a bit."

"No," Sam said. "He's still a pain in my ass."

Xander smiled. "And Sam still doesn't realize that the pain in her ass isn't me, it's the stick she has permanently lodged up there."

As the elevator rose, the three of them opened their briefcases, extracted their guns, and readied them for a fight.

Sarah said, "I don't think your charm will work on Maragos, Xander. So what's the plan here?"

"Yeah, you're probably right. We try to take him alive, but if we can't, we can't."

"I think you might have some sort of disorder, Xander," Sarah laughed. "Two totally different people."

Sam said, "So long as it's the super-soldier that shows up right now, you can have a hundred personalities, for all I care."

The elevator door dinged, and Xander held his pistol down by his side as he casually walked out. He made a right as Iliana directed, and at the far end of the hall was a fogged glass door. In the middle of it, in white lettering, all it said was INSURANCE. For a guy with the wherewithal to perfect nanobot technology, Gregor Maragos had zero imagination.

Xander approached the door. Sam and Sarah were ready at his heels. He peered through the fogged glass but saw nothing. Not even shadows moving back and forth. And the entire floor was completely silent. Only the faint buzz of traffic moving along just outside the building. Xander opened the door with his left hand and moved in with his gun extended in his right.

He walked into a small reception area. A few waiting chairs on the right as well as along the window in front of him, and an empty desk to his left. No sign of anyone. Xander glanced back and motioned toward the hallway to his right. The ladies nodded, following closely, their weapons ready. Xander walked toward the hallway entrance, his ears pricked, listening for any clue that someone was there. In the back of his brain the notion grew that they had somehow missed Maragos leaving the building. The fear of where he could be and what nasty attack he could be implementing at that very moment rose inside Xander.

For the first time since leaving the elevator, he heard a noise. It seemed to be coming from the back of the office building.

Ding.

Then quiet for a few seconds.

Ding.

Xander walked forward down the hall.

Ding.

There were office doors all along his right side, and the windows on his left looked out over downtown Athens.

Ding.

The ding was getting louder. All of the offices on his right were empty, nothing but walls and carpet. It was clear they were in the right place, but where the hell was Maragos?

Ding.

Xander was close enough to the dinging now so that in between each one he made out some sort of faint sliding noise, followed by a clunk.

Ding. Sliding. Clunk.

Xander looked back at Sam and Sarah. They were shadowing his movements, recognizing, like he did, that this empty office had never been used for an insurance agency.

Ding. Sliding. Clunk.

The repetitive noises were just around the corner from him now. The hallway turned right, and it was pretty clear to him that it was an elevator he was hearing. An elevator that was unable to close for some reason, but kept trying.

Ding. Sliding. Clunk.

Xander readied his Glock, sidled up to the wall of the last office before the turn in the hallway, then spun quickly out in the open, his gun extended. There was an elevator at the end of the hallway in front of him. It was open, a body lying face down at its threshold. Three more dead men slumped inside the elevator.

Ding.

The elevator signaled it was ready.

Sliding.

The doors began to shut.

Clunk.

The doors closed against the dead man's head and then slid back open.

Xander tucked his gun at the small of his back and moved forward.

"Looks like we were late to the party," he said to Sam and Sarah.

He approached the dead body, and Sam and Sarah filtered in behind him. He placed his hand against the door so it wouldn't close on the dead man's head again, tucked the toe of his oxford under the man's hip, and kicked up to roll him over.

"Gregor Maragos," Sarah gasped. "This is fantastic news."

Xander and Sam said in unison, "This is terrible news."

"Give me your phone," Xander told Sam.

She handed it to him.

"How is this bad?" Sarah said.

Xander dialed Marvin.

Sam answered Sarah. "It means we've chased down the wrong person. Someone else was running this thing. And now we are back to square one. The threat is still alive."

"Marvin, it's Xander. Maragos is dead."

"Xander, I'm with Director Hartsfield, can you repeat that? You're on speaker."

"Director, Maragos was already dead when we got to him. We were running down the wrong person."

Director Hartsfield answered, "How's that possible? Sarah heard his brother, Andonios, talk about Gregor building the weapon. Dbie Johnson has been working in the warehouse for weeks. She confirmed it was Gregor, and confirmed it was the nanobots that he'd built."

"I get all that, Mary," Xander said. "But clearly we're missing something. It's either Andonios who is—"

"No way," Sarah interrupted.

Xander ignored her. "It's either Andonios who is actually behind this or the American who's helped Gregor every step of the way."

"American?" Director Hartsfield was floored. "What are you talking about?"

Xander ignored her too. "Marvin, where are you on Ever-world Solutions? Who was hurt the most when the President shut the company down?"

"A lot of people lost a lot of money, but Congressman Jerry McDonnell definitely lost the most."

"Congressman?" Xander was annoyed but not surprised. Corruption ran deep. No one knew that more than Xander after finding out last year that then CIA Director William Manning was in Vitali Dragov's pocket. "Bring Jerry McDonnell in right now. Make him tell us what the hell is going on."

Mary spoke up. "Xander, you know I can't do that. He's a congressman. I can't just—"

"Lives depend on this, Mary. I know you understand that. Maybe even the life of the President!"

Mary was quiet for a moment.

Xander was frustrated. There were few things he hated more than bureaucracy.

Mary said, "I hear you, Xander. But I can't just bring in a congressman for questioning without any sort of proof of involvement. We aren't vigilantes here. We do have rules and protocols."

"Break them," Xander insisted.

"Xander—"

Xander removed the phone from his ear, started walking back down the hallway to leave, motioning for Sam and Sarah to come along.

He put the phone back to his ear. "Find out where Jerry McDonnell is, monitor him, tap his phones, his cars, hell, put a bug in his toilet for all I care, but we need to know every single move he makes. We're coming back to the States. Marvin, I need to know where this Doctor Kruger is. If she was his second in command, she'll know something. I need to know what she knows before I get back to the airport. You hear me?"

"I'll do my best, Xander."

The three of them got on the elevator.

"Just get it done. If we don't put all of this together in the next couple hours, we're going to be watching the news about another attack. I for one don't want that on my conscience. Do you?"

"Of course not, Xander," Mary replied.

"Figure it out!"

41

Mistaken Identity

XANDER, Sam, and Sarah boarded the jet back at Athens International Airport. Dbie Johnson was in the back plugging away on a laptop, and Kyle jumped up from his seat.

"I heard. Everyone okay?"

"Fine," Xander answered. "Maragos was dead when we got there. Nobody else was alive to give us trouble either. This is actually worst-case scenario."

"I thought the same thing," Kyle said. "Now what do we do?"

"We're heading back to the States. I'm hoping Marvin has some better info for us soon. Otherwise we'll just be chasing our tails when we do get back to America. Waiting for the next attack."

"So you think whoever killed Gregor will still want to go through with his agenda? You don't think it was about money? About owning the technology?"

Kyle made a good point. Someone could have killed Gregor

just to get him out of the way so they could make money. For Gregor this was about revenge. For his silent partner, it could have been more about the money. Xander hoped that was the case. If so, at least American lives would be safe for now. And if the congressman Jerry McDonnell was in fact the one silently involved with Gregor, they were already on the right track. The one loose end that kept nagging at Xander now was this Doctor Kruger. She just disappeared. And that made him nervous. Greek police raided her home just outside of Athens, and it was like no one lived there at all. It just didn't feel right.

"You could be right, Kyle," Xander finally answered. "It could be about the money. But we are still missing something. I can feel it. Where is the file on the Maragos family that the reporter left with us?"

Kyle said, "On the couch beside Dbie. I went back through it and couldn't find anything helpful, but give it a shot if you think you'll find something."

Xander walked to the back of the plane and sat beside Dbie. The engines fired up getting ready to take off for America.

"How's it coming, Dbie?" Xander asked as he opened the Maragos family file and began to thumb through it.

"Slow, but making progress. Faster than I thought initially, though, which is good."

"Good. What's the total?"

"I've been able to release the contents of six hundred nanobots. Whatever those little mosquitos had in their proboscis to inject in someone is now gone. A sting would be harmless."

"Great, keep at it. You're our only defense right now."

Dbie's face turned sorrowful. "I'm also the reason this is happening. I knew they were going to do something bad with this technology. I could just feel it. I wanted to quit making them, you have to believe me. When they hired me, I didn't know. I need the money—"

"It's all right, Dbie. You tried to tell the right people what was going on here when you found out. You risked your own life to do so, right? Hell, you even took a bullet for it."

Dbie didn't smile, but Xander could tell it was something she liked hearing.

"So tell me more about this Doctor Kruger?"

Dbie spoke as she plugged away on the laptop. "Not much to tell really. She said next to nothing, but she was always watching me close. Maybe she smelled 'traitor' on me. Why, you think she has something to do with this?"

"Hard to say. It's all really strange." Xander continued looking through the pages of the Maragos file. "There is nothing on her. No background, no information about where she's from or where she went to school, or jobs she's had. Nothing. We don't even know what she looks like."

Dbie glanced over at the pages Xander was looking through.

"Sure you do," she said.

Xander stopped and looked up at her, perplexed. "How's that?"

"You know what she looks like. You're looking right at her."

Xander looked down at the picture Dbie gestured toward. It wasn't computing.

Sam was eavesdropping close by, and when Dbie said those words, she rushed over to them from a few seats away. "Did I just hear you correctly?"

Dbie looked up at Sam, then back to Xander, who was still clearly confused. Then Dbie pointed at a photo sitting in Xander's lap. "That's her. That's Doctor Kruger."

Xander picked up the photo, giving Dbie a chance to see it more clearly. "This isn't Doctor Kruger," he said with confidence.

"Sure it is. Her hair might be a little different, but that's her all right. I think I would know. I worked for her for more than a few weeks. You don't forget a scowl like that."

Xander looked up at Sam. Sam's face was grim. "Call Marvin now. Get his team picking through every piece of video shot of anyone going in or out of this country in the last twenty-four hours."

Sam pulled her phone immediately. Kyle walked over to see what the commotion was about.

Xander asked Dbie, "When was the last time you saw Doctor Kruger?"

Dbie stopped typing on her laptop. "I guess last night before I quit. She wasn't around this morning like she normally is."

"You're *sure* you didn't see her this morning?"

"Yeah, I'm sure."

Kyle chimed in, "What's going on, X? You find something on Doctor Kruger?"

Xander held up the picture for Kyle to see.

"You could say that."

"What is it?" Kyle still didn't get it.

"Doctor Kruger isn't Doctor Kruger."

Xander pointed to the picture.

"She's Anastasia Maragos."

42

A Long Time Coming

THE WIND WHIPPED through the columns that stood to the left and right of her. She had the same view as Abraham Lincoln behind her. A view of the long rectangular reflecting pool. Fitting name, Anastasia thought, because it was reflecting the Washington Monument in its waters at that very moment. The trees that lined the pool were budding, and the pond off to her left was surrounded by blooming cherry blossoms. Amongst the trees and the tourists she would find a fine spot to enjoy the rest of the afternoon. A little relaxation before a very busy evening.

The glistening water in the pool just below the steps of the Lincoln Memorial reminded her of her childhood and the ocean waters she and her brother had been so fond of. Gregor had always been a strange sort. Father had always been more keen on Andonios, and Anastasia had always been Daddy's little girl. This left her brother to a lonely upbringing. Always in another's shadow, never the light their father ever saw.

But Gregor was always smarter than everybody else. Mostly because he grew up with a book permanently fixed in his hands. This left him falling short in the social interaction category. His lack of time with others made his social habits awkward. He hadn't a clue how to talk to strangers. And certainly no idea how to speak to women. All of this left him cold, alone in his own dark world. When the time was right, Anastasia was able to use this to manipulate him to do her bidding. The key for her was to make Gregor feel like he was the one in charge. It was something he'd never felt before, so giving him a little control, especially over a sister who had enjoyed father's favor, was like giving him the keys to the kingdom.

Just as she thought it might, it all went to his head. He did a fantastic job getting the nanotechnology right. But as with any recluse who didn't know the ins and outs of the human mind, he became paranoid. Not that there wasn't reason. Dbie Johnson had gone against them and contacted authorities. But it was his handling of the situation that had stained the otherwise clean operation she had managed to get him to build. The last week had been disastrous for her brother. Unfortunately for him, Anastasia knew he was only going to make it worse, so she had to shut him down. And she wouldn't miss him. Managing and coddling him had become a full-time job all on its own.

No longer having to wrangle Gregor, Andonios and Anastasia Maragos were now free to run this thing without an anchor pulling them down. Gregor had served his purpose. Without him *none* of this would have been possible. But now they could drop the act and get down to business. The time it took for her to keep Gregor in line and the time it took for Andonios to play the clue-less playboy brother was almost too much. But it had been worth it. It had enabled Gregor to perform at his peak, and ultimately it had allowed Anastasia and Andonios to obtain the perfect weapon.

Anastasia closed her eyes and let the breeze carrying the

scent from the cherry blossoms blow over her. This calm before the storm was needed. She hadn't had a lot of time for reflection the past few weeks. She let her mind drift. Because it was drilled into her head by her father, her thoughts always centered on having an inventory of money. Money was great. The Maragos family had always had money. And enough of it, she was taught, could also bring you a certain amount of power. But not *real* power. *Real* power came from being able to change the course of history. Something Anastasia and Andonios had been learning and studying since they were children. A man like Leo Maragos doesn't make the kind of money he makes by spending a lot of time with his family. That meant others had to step in and help raise Anastasia and her brothers. Anastasia was so happy that had been the case, because she got to learn about other things besides the almighty dollar. She felt fortunate that, unlike most children who grow up billionaires, she and Andonios had a sense of purpose in their lives.

Anastasia would never forget the day she met Majid Hammoud. That day shaped the rest of her life. When Anastasia was seven years old, the Maragos family brought a full-time nanny into their home. Lubena was a wonderfully caring woman. She took care of the Maragos children in every way, teaching them many great and useful things. But it was her husband, Majid, who taught them about the world. They would spend every Sunday at Lubena and Majid's home. It was a shoebox compared to where Anastasia and her brothers lived, but it was full of life. The Hammouds had two sons of their own, the same age as Anastasia and Gregor.

After Sunday dinner, always a meal common in their Lebanese culture, Majid would gather the children and tell them stories of Allah, and all about how the Western world had gone astray. Leading the world's culture down a dark and dangerous path. He would look at Anastasia and her brothers sternly and tell them it was up to *us* to be the change Allah wants to see in the world.

Every day, ever since the day that Majid was killed by American soldiers in Lebanon as he was rallying Allah's children, Anastasia, her brother Andonios, and Majid's sons, Saajid and Husaam Hammoud, had been patiently waiting and planning for a day like today to come. It had been a long and difficult journey, but phase one of their plan was finally about to commence.

Anastasia's burner phone began to ring. She knew it would be Andonios checking up on her.

"Hello."

"Are you safe?"

"I am, Andonios. I told you not to worry. Where are you?"

"London."

"Good, you'll be getting started soon?"

"I will. Have you heard from Saajid or Husaam?"

Anastasia knew Andonios was hurting, so she left out any details. "I have."

"Gregor didn't have to die, Anastasia. I could have kept him under control."

"Andonios. I have been working right beside him for weeks, and even I couldn't control him. We didn't have time to babysit. What we are doing is far too important. You know that many sacrifices must be made to enact true change."

"Why must we always be the ones to sacrifice? Answer that, Anastasia. Father wasn't enough? Now our brother? When does it stop? Am I next? Are you?"

Andonios was always the softer of the two of them. She needed to play to his sensibility, make him think she understood. Just the way Gregor thought he was when Andonios was just playing along.

"Listen, brother. If I am next, it is a necessary sacrifice. This means far more than our own lives. You know this. And we aren't the only ones to sacrifice. Have you already forgotten? Saajid and Husaam lost their father many years ago for this cause. Is it not as important for you as it needs to be?"

"Do not question my resolve." Some of the metal had returned to Andonios's voice. Anastasia liked hearing this.

"Then point your anger in the right direction. Gregor's death is not because of us. It is because of the Western movement that is swallowing our children's future. We must stop them—"

Andonios interrupted. "You don't have to tell me why we are doing this. I believe as you believe. As Majid taught us to believe."

"No, Andonios. As Allah teaches us to believe."

Silence.

"I must go," Anastasia said. "I will be in touch tonight when it is done."

She ended the call. She took one last look behind her at Abraham Lincoln. She couldn't help but feel as though he would be disappointed if he knew what his America had turned into. She walked out of the security camera's view, dropped her red hijab that covered her entire body, and tucked her suitcase into the dark corner where one of her associates would later pick it up and put everything where it needed to be for the evening. She then walked down the steps, back toward her command center that was already set up for her to do her work. It was time to prepare. On her walk to the Washington Monument, she had a phone conversation with Saajid. It focused her. The Americans were hot on her trail. He told her that the man named Xander King, whom she had told Gregor to have eliminated, had been to the office building where Saajid had killed her brother. And that Xander and his team had already left the airport in Athens.

Unlike Gregor, she welcomed this American agent and his team. They were one of the biggest reasons America had been able to flourish. Because of soldiers like King fighting so valiantly,

Western culture had spread like a cancer. Yes, she welcomed them back to America. Because she had something very specific ready for them when they landed. This is why she wasn't worried about them at all.

43

Clear the Air

THE EIGHT-AND-A-HALF-HOUR FLIGHT back to Washington, DC, had been brutal. Xander's mind had been in overdrive the entire time. He needed to rest, but it had proved impossible. They left Athens at three thirty in the afternoon, so after the time change it was still only five o'clock in DC. Most of the teens involved in the incident at the Acropolis were now dead. The media was reporting that there are zero leads in finding who was responsible. However, the plane ride had brought Xander and team quite a bit of clarity in that regard.

Clarifying moment number one came even before takeoff, when Dbie figured out Doctor Kruger to be Anastasia Maragos. And while they still didn't know where Anastasia was, at least they knew who they were looking for. That put them far ahead of where they were when they left a dead Gregor lying in the elevator in Athens.

Clarifying moment number two was a break in tracking

down Anastasia's help in America. Unfortunately, Marvin was so far unable to track the money being fed into the shell company, Rig's Recycling. However, Marvin had found a link between Congressman Jerry McDonnell, Everworld Solutions, and communication between a Greek phone number and a cell phone bought in McDonnell's name less than a year ago. The Greek number was uncertain, but to Xander that was a moot point. The coincidence was far too large for Jerry not to have been working back channels for Maragos, likely getting him the materials he needed to build the nanobots. The calls were recent as well. If they could track down where the phone was the next time it was used, it would be a bingo.

The last important tie-in was to speak to the President about Congressman McDonnell. If Jerry had been the one behind buying up Leo Maragos's properties, and bringing all the negative attention to Everworld, they would know for certain Jerry had been the silent partner in this massive undertaking. And at the very least it would be enough to bring him in and make him spill what he knows. As soon as Xander could get to the White House, he and the President could clear things up about Jerry.

The key in all of this now lay in finding Anastasia. Somehow she had slipped through the cracks. Playing Doctor Kruger was smart. She needed a way to see what Gregor was doing, but she had to remain obscure if someone like Dbie happened to leak it out. Xander's team was fortunate Sarah had been able to get Dbie out of there alive. Dbie worked tirelessly on the plane ride. She managed to take down 1,600 more nanobots. That made 2,400 total, leaving 1,600 still active, at least of those they knew about.

The plane finally touched down in DC. Sam had cars waiting for them, ready to get them to the White House as quickly as possible. As they were taxiing to the waiting vehicles, Sam's phone rang.

"It's Marv," Sam said. She put the call on speaker. "We're all listening, Marv."

"Our software hit a match."

Everyone closed in around Sam to hear the news.

"Where is she?" Xander asked.

"You made the right call coming back to the States, X. She's here. Security cameras picked her up this morning arriving at the Washington Dulles Airport right here in DC."

"Shit, this is bad." Xander stood from his seat. A pit formed in his stomach.

"I know. I have alerted all authorities, and they are doing their best to dispatch anyone and everyone to find her."

"What else do we know?" Sam asked.

"She took a taxi straight to the Washington Monument. One large suitcase. We've been combing through camera footage. But we haven't been able to pick her back up."

"What do you mean? There are cameras everywhere in that area," Xander said, irritated.

"She must have known this as well. We lost her in a blind spot at the Lincoln Memorial. She sat on the steps for a while, even took a couple calls, then when she got up, she walked out of camera shot and we never picked her up again. And she isn't still there, I had a ranger go and check. She's just gone. Someone has to be helping her."

Xander was pissed. This could be the difference in saving many lives, and they let her get away. But he didn't say anything. He knew she was working with someone in the US, and he couldn't help but wonder if it was someone other than just an old congressman.

"Find her, Marv."

"I'm on it."

Sam ended the call.

"Dbie, you and Bob are going to stay right here on the plane, okay?

Dbie looked up from her laptop and gave Xander a nod.

"Keep plugging away. I'll have some security stay behind and watch the plane. You should have everything you need right here."

The plane came to a stop, and Bob shut down the engines.

"The rest of you come with me. Sarah, coordinate with Marvin. I want whoever is leading the search to run everything by you. That way you can filter what's important and relay it to us. When you and Kyle get separated from Sam and me at the White House, remember to call Sam with anything important. I don't have my phone."

"Got it," Sarah said.

The door opened and the stairs lowered to the ground. Xander walked down and was greeted by a CIA agent. The young, muscular man shook Xander's hand.

"Mr. King, Agent John Karn. We have an SUV ready to take you to the White House. The President is waiting to speak with you there. I have a three-person detail to remain here at the plane to guard Ms. Johnson as she works."

Marv was on top of things.

"Okay. Let's get out of here then."

Xander took a few steps toward the row of blacked-out SUVs, following Agent Karn's lead. When he looked back to make sure his team—his friends—were following behind him, the moment that would change his life forever happened in an instant. And there was nothing he, one of the greatest soldiers in the history of the United States military, could do but watch in horror.

44

Reality Bites . . . Or Stings

WHEN XANDER TURNED from following Agent Karn, everything happened in slow motion. In more than ten years of navigating intense battle situations, Xander had seen the most frightening things any human could witness. Bombs blowing off limbs, bullets tearing through heads, the blade of his own knife slicing right through a throat, more violence than fifty lifetimes. But this . . . this was far worse. He had never been more terrified in his entire life.

The sun was going down, but it was still plenty bright to illuminate the horrible scene. There were no gunshots. No bombs exploding. No sign of danger whatsoever. But when Xander saw Sam cringe and slap at her neck like she was swatting a fly, everything in Xander screamed in panic.

"GET DOWN!" His shout echoed across the tarmac.

But it was too late.

He watched as Sarah slapped away at the air, spinning to get away from an invisible attack.

Then it was Kyle's turn. Xander tried to run toward him. To tackle him. To do *something*. But it was no use. He watched as his closest friend in all the world, his brother since grade school, swatted at his neck. Kyle looked shocked as he cupped his hand over his bare skin.

"Kyle!" Xander shouted.

Then he felt arms wrap around him, someone else's momentum carrying him to the ground. It was Sam. She landed on top of him and tried to act as a protective blanket.

"Pull your arms underneath me, Xander. Don't move!"

"What's happening?" Dbie shouted from the jet's doorway.

Kyle turned toward her, still in shock. "I think we just got stung."

Dbie bolted down the stairs and rushed to Kyle's side.

"Let me up, Sam." Xander needed to act.

"Don't move, Xander. If she sent those things for us, she sent one for you as well."

Xander didn't care. He lifted Sam off him and jumped to his feet.

"Xander!" Sam shouted.

He turned to her, concerned. "Where was it? Where did it sting you?"

Sam was defiant. "Just get back on the plane and shut the door, Xander. Now, before you get stung!"

Xander grabbed her by the arm and yanked her toward the plane. "Everyone! Inside now! Agent Karn, get your team back in the SUVs and wait for my order!"

Sarah rushed up the stairs, Dbie and Kyle followed, and Bob shut the door as soon as Xander and Sam were in. Xander immediately turned to Dbie.

"How will we know if these were some of the nanobots you

emptied?" He gave a sweeping look over all of his loved ones. "How will we know if they are safe?"

Dbie had a faraway look on her face.

"Dbie! How?"

Xander's shout snapped her out of it.

"I-I would need the nanobot that stung them. At least one of them."

Xander turned to Bob. "Open the door."

"No, Xander!" Sam stepped in and grabbed his arm. "You can't go out there. Don't be stupid."

Bob waited.

"Open the door, Bob. And shut it as soon as I'm down."

"Xander!" Sarah shouted.

Xander ripped his arm from Sam's grasp and rushed down the steps to the tarmac. Bob shut the door behind him. As the others looked on from inside the plane, Xander began to scour the blacktop. Agent Karn stepped out of one of the SUVs.

"Agent Karn! Get over here!"

Karn ran over. "What's going on, what happened?"

"I'm looking for a mosquito-sized robot. Call your men over and help us search."

"Like the ones in Athens? They're here now?"

Xander looked up. "They're here. And I need to find one that stung my partners."

Karn did as Xander asked, but they didn't need any more help. Lying on a yellow stripe on the ground Xander found what looked like a tiny rock. When he moved closer, he saw it was a nanobot. He picked it up by its wings between his index finger and thumb, astonished by how small yet how lifelike it was. He looked up into the windows of the plane and nodded his head. The door opened and Xander ascended the stairs.

"Got one," Xander handed it to Dbie.

She took it carefully from him, being sure to prevent the proboscis from touching her. "This will take a few minutes,

Xander. But we really should go ahead and get them to a hospital."

Xander poked his head outside the airplane door.

"Agent Karn, get a car ready to take us to the nearest hospital."

Karn nodded and grabbed his phone.

"Why wasn't I stung?" Xander said aloud.

Xander's skin was crawling. As he looked at three of his favorite people on the planet, all in the worst kind of danger, there was nothing he could do about it. He became angry.

"Why them and not me, Dbie?"

"Give her a moment, Xander," Sam said. "It's not her fault. And it's not yours."

Dbie plugged away at her computer, intermittently inspecting the nanobot.

Xander looked at Kyle, then Sarah. "Do you all feel okay? Do you feel anything?"

"We're okay, Xander," Kyle said.

"I feel fine. I'm not even sure I was stung. I just heard something buzz by my ear. I'm sure it's okay," Sarah said, trying to comfort him.

"How did they know to go directly to them and sting them, Dbie?"

Xander couldn't wait. It was eating him alive.

Dbie looked up. "Doctor Kruger—or I guess Gregor's sister, Anastasia—must have somehow gotten ahold of their cell phone numbers."

It hit Sam. "That's why you weren't stung, Xander. You don't have your cell phone."

Xander couldn't believe it. Submerging his phone at the marina in Santorini had saved him from the same fate as his friends. This made him even angrier. Why them and not him? Maybe it's okay. Maybe these were some of the nanobots that Dbie was able to—

"Shit."

Xander looked up and his heart dropped. The way Dbie said the word, coupled by the worried look on her face, was all Xander needed to hear. It was all he needed to understand that his friends, even though they felt fine, were dying.

Dbie let everyone in on what Xander already knew.

"The nanobots were active. I'm so sorry. We have to get them to the hospital. Now."

45

Revelations

THE THREE-SUV CARAVAN weaved in and out of rush hour traffic as best they could. The roads were slammed. They used the shoulders whenever possible, even veering off-road when necessary. Xander, Kyle, Sam, and Sarah were in the middle SUV. Xander had never been so nervous. He kept expecting at any moment that symptoms would start to permeate any or all of their systems. So far there was nothing.

"You're sure you feel fine?" Xander asked them.

Kyle answered for the group. "I feel completely normal."

The rest of them agreed.

"Xander, we need to get to the White House and speak with the President. All of us are fine. At least let Sarah and Kyle go ahead to the hospital while you and I—"

"It's not happening, Sam. You all are going to the hospital to be monitored. I'll go to the White House after I know you're being properly cared for."

Sam was insistent. "Xander, there is no time for this. The White House is all the way across town. In this traffic it could take you more than an hour. I know you care about us, but there are bigger things at stake here. You know this."

Xander shook his head. "But what can I do right now anyway? They don't know where Anastasia is."

"Right, but if President Williams knows anything more about Jerry McDonnell, you can bring him in and make him talk. Maybe Jerry has been communicating with Anastasia. You heard Marvin, someone from the States has been in contact with a Greek number that was triangulated to the Washington Monument. That isn't a coincidence."

Xander didn't speak. The SUVs swerved around more traffic. He felt helpless. He could do nothing for his friends, and he could do nothing to help protect his country. Something had to give, or they were all in trouble.

Sam's phone rang.

"It's a DC number," she said.

Xander took the phone from her. "Hello?"

"This is Brandon Sizemore, director of the Secret Service. I need to speak with Xander King."

There was a note of panic in his voice, which in turn sparked panic in Xander.

"This is him. Is the President okay?"

"For now, but *all* of my men guarding the perimeter of the White House are down."

"Down?"

"Down. Dropped to the ground, not responding."

"What the hell are you calling me for?" Xander didn't understand. "Have you followed protocol?"

"Yes, we are in the emergency operations center now. But, Xander, I am calling because there is no other protocol. We are under attack. But there is nothing to shoot at."

The nanobots.

Anastasia Maragos's plan had been put into action. And she was coming for the President.

Sizemore continued, "What the hell are we dealing with here, King? How do we stop it?"

"I don't know. But tell the President I'm on my way."

He ended the call and immediately dialed his jet's phone, putting the call on speaker so everyone could hear.

"What's going on, Xander?" Sam asked.

Xander ignored her. He tapped on the driver's shoulder. "Stop the car."

Agent Karn turned to face him from the front passenger seat.

"Agent Karn," Xander said. The jet's phone began to ring. "You have military experience?"

"Marines, sir."

"Combat?"

"Two tours in Iraq, one in Afghanistan, sir."

"You ready for one more mission?"

"Anything you need, sir."

"You and I are taking one of these trucks. Make sure the other two get my team to the hospital."

Agent Karn said, "Yes, sir. Where can I tell Director Hartsfield we are going?"

"You can't, because I don't know yet."

Agent Karn didn't ask another question. He radioed the other vehicles.

Bob answered the phone on the jet. "Everything all right, Xander?"

The SUVs came to a stop on the side of the busy road.

"Put Dbie on the phone."

As soon as the director of the Secret Service said there was nothing to shoot at, something clicked for Xander. He couldn't believe he hadn't thought of it before.

"Xander, I'm glad you called," Dbie answered. "The last group of fifty nanobots I took offline were at the White House. The

White House! I can't take them down fast enough. They're going to get inside!"

"Dbie, take a breath," Xander said, calm. "I don't want you to take them down."

Sam, Kyle, and Sarah all looked at Xander in shock. Had he lost his mind?

"W-what? I can't . . . This is the only way to stop them!"

"I don't think it is."

Sam couldn't hold her tongue. "Xander, what are you doing? We can't stop her from—"

Xander held up his index finger.

"I don't understand," Dbie said.

"You built in a back door to these nanobots, right? So you can get access to them?"

"Right, that's how I'm shutting them down."

"I want you to stop shutting them down."

Kyle spoke up as Xander got out of the SUV. "What the hell, X! They're at the White House. The President is in danger."

Xander covered the phone and spoke to the three of them.

"Will you let me finish this call?"

They were quiet, all visibly worried.

Dbie sounded confused. "I can't, Xander. I have to keep working on this."

"I didn't say stop working on it, Dbie. I said stop shutting them down. Now, I don't know a damn thing about this technology, but if you have access to the nanobots' systems, can't you see who else does too?"

Sam and Sarah sat forward. A look of hope flashed in their eyes.

Dbie was thinking. "Well . . . no. I wouldn't know exactly who was controlling them . . ."

The hope left the faces of Sam and Sarah as quickly as it had appeared. Xander felt the last of his hope flicker as well.

"But . . ."

There was a *but*.

"But what, Dbie?" Xander said impatiently.

"But . . . I'll be damned if I can't trace *where* the controlling signal is coming from."

Sam, Kyle, and Sarah silently rejoiced inside the vehicle. Xander had a silent sigh of relief himself.

"Find the signal. I'll call you back in just a minute."

"I'm on it."

Xander ended the call and gave Sam back her phone.

"Brilliant work, Xander," Sam said.

"We'll see . . . *if* she can locate the signal's location." He turned to the driver. "Get them to the hospital right away."

"Yes, sir."

"Xander, I'm coming with you," Sam said.

"You're not." He put his hands on her shoulders as she tried to exit the SUV. "You heard Dbie, those bots that stung you were active. I know you are the most bullheaded human on the planet—"

"You're one to talk."

"But you are going to that hospital, Sam." He looked around the SUV. "All of you are. You are the most important people in the world to me, and I can't lose you. I'll do whatever it takes to keep you alive."

Xander had no idea the depths those words would carry in the coming hours.

"Sam, he's right," Kyle said. "I want to go fight this thing too, but we can't do anything if we're dead."

"It's not up for debate," Xander said. "You're going to the hospital. The White House is under attack right now, by forces we've never fought before. I have to go."

"That is why we have to come with you." Sam was adamant. "We have to figure out how to fight these things with you."

"Not this time, Sam. Besides, when Dbie gives me the location of where these bots are being controlled—where Anastasia

Maragos is—I know exactly how to fight that. I don't need to fight the nanobots."

Sam said. "Wherever she is, she will be guarded."

Xander looked over at Agent Karn. "I've got a combat Marine with me. I like my odds."

Agent Karn agreed. "Oorah."

46

Don't Forget the Popcorn

SENATOR GRAHAM THOMAS paced the floor of his living room. It had been most of the day since he heard from Anastasia Maragos. Since he'd had any update at all. This was the exact reason he put the recycling company in Athens in her husband's name without anyone knowing. No matter what happened, the blow-back would always be tied back to them. To her. He thought it was brilliant the way she handled her crazy brother, but he wasn't sure she could pull this thing off. This was the way it had to be, though. If he were any more hands-on, he too could be implicated. Part of the reward of removing himself was being able to stay invisible if things went wrong. But that didn't make it easy for him to sit back and watch. Hell, he couldn't even watch: he was entirely in the dark.

For about the fiftieth time of the hour, he dialed Anastasia's new burner phone.

"Would you stop calling me!" Anastasia shouted at him through the phone. "I don't have time for this!"

"I have called you fifty times. Fifty! What the hell is going on?"

"You changed your phone but did not give me the number. I didn't want to answer if it wasn't you."

"Bullshit. Now what the hell is going on?"

"I don't answer to you, Senator. The plan is in motion. Do not call me again."

"What about Jerry McDonnell? You can't forget about him. He is the loose end that will take us all down."

Anastasia sighed, annoyed. Graham's blood was boiling. He had gone to great lengths earlier in the day, putting himself at massive risk, to plant the cell phone in Jerry's briefcase which he himself had been using to talk to Anastasia. He knew they would investigate the money trail and it would lead back to his old friend. And he knew that if push came to shove, his old friend Jerry would rat him out. The phone would tie Jerry to Anastasia nicely, but he would still tell investigators that Graham was the one actually pulling the strings. If Jerry died before he could talk, the investigation would stop with him. The evidence Graham had put together made sure of that.

"Look, I will not say this again. I am busy. I cannot have any more distractions. Have you turned on the television? The White House is under attack. You realize this takes great concentration. Breaking through the security and the walls of the White House?!" She was shouting, but then she went calm. "I will have my bots inside in a matter of minutes. And as for the rest of these questions, I have cleaned up *all* of your messes for you, Senator. I have a bot tracking to Jerry McDonnell's cell phone as we speak, he will be dead soon as well. And I have already taken care of the clandestine team that has been trying to run us down. No thanks to you. I had nanobots waiting for them when they landed here in Washington. That is, if the cell numbers you gave me for them were correct."

Graham couldn't help but smile. Everything was coming together perfectly.

"The numbers were correct."

"Goodbye, Senator."

Anastasia ended the call.

Graham went over to the bar and poured a celebratory scotch. It would be good to sip on as he watched the show. He walked around the couch and flipped on the television above the fireplace. The news was reporting in front of the White House, but from a much farther distance than usual. The reporter was frantic. The perimeter was down, and what looked like a large swarm of insects was moving in a dark cloud in front of the White House.

Graham took a sip of his scotch. He couldn't believe it. More than a year of diligent work had paid off. The stuff of science fiction was knocking on the President's door. Meticulous planning had made it all happen.

"And now the *President*," he said to the empty room with great disdain, "will finally get his due."

The millions of dollars that the President cost him by shutting down Everworld Solutions was going to pale in comparison to the billions these little weapons and their technology would bring. He already had a black market bidding war brewing. Not easy with something so top secret. But one thing you can count on, even with the nastiest criminals on Earth, is that the promise of absolute power can keep every mouth shut. And that is exactly what this nanobot technology offered: billions to Graham and absolute power to whoever paid him for it.

He took another sip of his scotch and let it settle over him during this proud moment. All that he had accomplished so far was brilliant, but a smile grew over his face with the thought of the last piece of his ingenious puzzle: his meeting with Andonios Maragos, the best meeting he had ever had.

He had played their entire family like a fiddle. Anastasia was the leader, that much was easy to tell after one conversation with Gregor. They feigned estrangement to the public just so an operation like this couldn't be tied to all of them. But Gregor spilled that info after Graham got him excited about the materials he could supply. Once Graham got his hooks in Anastasia, the toughest of the bunch, making her realize she needed him, Andonios was easy. But for Graham, Andonios was the most important piece of the puzzle.

Graham knew if they could actually pull off perfecting nanobot technology, Anastasia would only want it for herself. Gregor had explained that Anastasia's only motivation was revenge on the President for making her father kill himself. Graham didn't buy it, but it didn't matter, because the President dying would be a bonus for him. He knew the key for him to gain access to the technology in order to sell it lay in the greedy hands of Andonios. Andonios was resistant at first, telling Graham what he already knew about his sister's motivations. But when Graham began giving Andonios figures, how much he could *actually* make, Andonios agreed to hand over a copy of all the blueprints of the technology.

Anastasia would never let that fly of course, so she too would have to disappear. Easy, Graham figured; she may have security, but when the US military pegged her as the one responsible for the death of the President, Graham wouldn't have to lift a finger. They would hunt her to the ends of the earth.

It was the perfect plan.

The action on the television was ramping up, and Graham just sat back and enjoyed the show.

47

Call Me Crazy

"Xander, I found her."

Dbie's voice finally came through the speaker of Agent Karn's phone after nearly five minutes of silence. John Karn and Xander had already broken away from the others who were headed to the ER. John was doing a good job of getting around traffic on their way to the White House. Xander unchecked the mute button.

"We are close to the White House, heading west. Are we going the right way?"

"You are. The signal is coming from a townhouse in Dupont Circle. Only about a mile northwest of the White House. I'll text you the exact address."

"Good work, Dbie."

"I'll check security cameras on the road to see if I can tell you what the situation is outside. Would you like me to cut the power? Might give you an advantage."

"Dbie, is there something I don't know about your background?"

"Yeah, I got bored at MIT and did some work for a private investigator."

"That's handy. But listen, don't worry about any of that. You get back to shutting down the nanobots. I'll have Marvin work on those things you mentioned. Stay at it, Dbie. You are saving a lot of lives."

"I won't stop until this is over. Good luck, Xander."

Xander ended the call and gave John the address to put in the GPS. He then texted Marv the address to the townhouse where the signal controlling the nanobots was coming from, and asked him to be ready to cut the power and go ahead and check the cameras. Dbie Johnson may have had a hand in building these little monsters, but they would never have been able to have a chance at stopping them without her. For that he was grateful. Instead of texting back, Marv was calling in on John's phone.

"Marv, you got my text?"

"Got it, and my team is on it. But Xander, I have Anastasia Maragos on the phone. She wants to talk to you. And you alone. Shall I patch her through?"

Xander didn't know what to think about her calling him. It could mean a lot of things, maybe even the fact that she wanted to negotiate a way out.

"Interesting. Put her through."

Marvin asked, "You want us on the call?"

"No. It's best no one hears what I'm about to say to her."

"Your call. Patching her through."

Xander cleared his throat and tried to prepare himself for anything.

He heard a click on the line. He took the phone off speaker and put it to his ear. John continued weaving around traffic. The sun was dropping below the horizon as dusk settled in.

Xander covered the phone. "John, do you have any headphones you can plug into the car stereo? This is a confidential call."

"Of course," John said.

Xander watched as he pulled some earbuds from the console, plugged them into the car stereo, and turned up the volume loud enough for Xander to hear the music coming from his ears.

"Are we secure?" A woman's voice came on the line.

"We are. What the hell do you want, Anastasia?"

"You're sure we are alone."

"Spit it out," Xander growled.

"All right. Straight to business then. First, congratulations on surviving my nanobot. I checked its camera footage, it seems it didn't have any place to go. I'm not sure if you left your phone turned off by luck or on purpose, but either way, it saved your life."

Xander's mind flashed to when he turned and saw Sam slap away the nanobot that had stung her just outside the jet. He felt sick. If a bot was sent to *kill* him, then the bots that stung his team must have been sent to kill as well.

"And it will end yours," Xander said matter-of-factly.

"Is that what you think? I beg to differ. You see, I also checked the cameras on the other bots, and they were quite successful at hitting their targets. All of them. Do your friends seem sick in any way?"

Xander didn't answer.

"Well, they won't. Not until I want them to."

"What is this call about, Anastasia? Why are you targeting the President? You think he had something to do with your father's death?"

Anastasia laughed. "You are naïve, Mr. King. I would expect different from someone who has seen so much war. This is much bigger than my father, and my brother as well. They were necessary sacrifices for the greater good."

Greater good? Anastasia was starting to sound like an Islamic extremist. Like this war she was waging was more than just about her family. Like it was about more than revenge. Xander hadn't seen this coming.

"So it isn't about revenge," he said. "And it isn't about money. Why are you doing this? There's no way you can win."

Anastasia didn't take the bait.

"I've already won. The fear of my little creations is enough alone to show that the United States' war machine no longer holds its power. And as far as *why* I'm doing this? That is of no concern to you. And it's just like you Americans to think this is a competition to win."

Again, she was sounding much more like someone with a grudge against the entire country. This was not good.

"But I will be honest. The *what* in this equation *is* a concern to me. And the *what* is you."

Xander let her speak. They were only a few minutes from her hiding place in the townhouse.

"You have managed to be a pain in my ass for days now. A cat with nine lives, if you will. And I did some research on you and how well you have done fighting what America calls the 'war on terror.' Ironic when the rest of the world knows that America is the true terror."

Xander interrupted, "There a point to this story? I have some little machines to destroy."

"This is my point. Soldiers like you are perpetuating the putrid American culture that is ruining our world."

"Our world? American culture? Am I talking to the daughter of a Greek billionaire? Or the daughter of Osama Bin Laden?"

"Keep joking, Xander." Her tone grew colder. "But I'm tired of talking. I know you are coming after me. And you might find me. So listen very closely to what I am saying. Am I coming in clear?"

Xander swallowed his pride and let her continue to talk down to him.

"Crystal clear."

"Good. Because I don't have a lot of time. I've just made my way inside the White House."

Xander didn't give her the satisfaction of a response. He just hoped she hadn't actually managed to get those little bastards inside.

Anastasia continued, "I have injected your friends with nanochips. Are you familiar?"

Xander's blood ran cold. He was familiar. They were microchips small enough to fit into your bloodstream. The military had been using a form of them for years to monitor targets from anywhere in the world.

"I am familiar." He could barely speak.

"There is only one way that your friends make it out of this alive. One. Way."

Xander attempted a deep breath but could only manage a couple small ones.

"I'm listening. How do they make it out of this alive, Anastasia?"

The rest of the conversation with Anastasia Maragos was a blur. He felt as if he were watching it from someone else's body. Though what she said in those few moments could not be ignored, it could also not be his focus. He had no choice but to put it out of his mind completely until he could reach her. Until he could end this thing once and for all.

48

Worse Than It Sounds

JOHN'S PHONE began to ring in Xander's lap. He had all of ten seconds to feel sorry for himself after the worst phone conversation he'd ever had. He knew this was the life he chose a long time ago, and somewhere in the back of his mind, he knew this day would come. So he put out of his mind what he couldn't control, and turned to do what every soldier is trained to do: complete the mission.

With a deep breath, he refocused.

Save the President.

He motioned that John could remove his headphones and answered the incoming call. "How's it looking, Marv?"

"Not good. Just got word that the White House has been breached. The nanobots are inside."

Anastasia was a lot of things, but it seems liar wasn't one of them.

"Yeah, I heard. What's the likelihood they can get to the President?"

"Not likely, but I don't know exactly their capabilities."

Xander said, "Just make sure all outside air supply is cut off to the PEOC."

"It's all independent, no way even something as small as a mosquito can get in there. But that isn't the problem."

"I know," Xander said. "It's finding all the nanobots and making certain they can't harm anyone. They're so small, Anastasia could hide them anywhere in there. Behind paintings, cabinets, you get the point."

"Right. I think Dbie will be able to tell us that, but we won't know for sure until she's finished. Which will be hours."

"How many people are inside the White House?"

Marv let out a sigh. "Three hundred and forty-two, unsecured. There was a press briefing. It was a mistake."

"Damn it."

Xander took the phone away from his ear. Anastasia would kill every last one of them. Finding her and killing her, fast, was the only way to save these people. And possibly a lot more. Whether or not she killed the President, she was right when she said she had already won. Given what these nanobots could do, actually breaching the White House, how could anyone ever feel safe again?

"Listen, Marv, keep this between us."

"Of course."

"This is a lot worse than it sounds."

"I'm not sure that is possible, Xander."

"It is. Kyle, Sam, and Sarah have all been injected with nanochips. Anastasia was more than happy to let me know that when signaled the chips will burst the capsule in their bloodstream."

"Okay." Marv sounded nervous.

"Marv, it's marburg virus. I don't know where Anastasia got

the strain, but the capsules are filled with marburg. Even worse, she said it's been coupled with influenza."

"Marburg is like an even deadlier ebola. Xander, there's a chance this could spread. If the influenza germs carry the marburg, it could be airborne."

"That's why I said it's a lot worse. You need to get the CDC to those who are dead or dying around the White House. Though I believe the security outside was injected with poison instead of marburg. That's why they are already down. Anastasia thought this all the way through. I have to stop her before it gets even worse."

"I'll put the CDC on alert and make sure everyone is moved as far away from the White House as possible. As for Anastasia, I'm looking at the front of the townhouse where Dbie directed us. There is some pedestrian foot traffic, making it difficult to distinguish who is who, but there is definitely a suspicious car. Two men have been sitting in a white Toyota Camry for as long as I've been watching. I've only been able to scan back an hour, but I did see two other men go inside the townhouse. I'm trying to get a drone overhead to pick up infrared to let you know how many are inside, but it's going to be a few minutes."

"I don't have a few minutes. We are pulling into the neighborhood now."

"That's all I've got," Marv said.

"I'll call or text to let you know when to cut the power when John and I are headed inside."

"Copy that."

"Marv, have Director Hartsfield call this phone in five minutes. If I don't answer, I'll call her right back. It's important."

"You got it."

Xander didn't mention the reason he needed to speak with the director of the CIA at such an inopportune time. He also didn't mention the last part of the conversation with Anastasia for the same reason. But he couldn't keep a part of what she'd said from repeating in his mind:

"How about your sister? Would be a shame for your niece to grow up without a mother."

His adrenaline spiked again, the way it had when she first said it.

"You better watch your mouth," he had shouted at her.

Anastasia was cold as ice. "I think you'd better watch yours. When's the last time you spoke with her?"

"If you touch my sister—"

"I wonder if she's had any mosquito bites recently? Say, in the last hour . . ."

Xander remembered how he couldn't breathe when Anastasia told him she'd sent a nanobot to Helen. Not only was his team—his friends—in danger, but his sister? It was all too much.

Anastasia had told him what she needed from him to keep them all safe. He already knew what he had to do, but he figured the five minutes he gave himself before Mary called him would be long enough to second-guess himself. But he knew it wouldn't change anything. He took a deep breath and slid John's phone in his pocket.

John said, "I think we should park here. The townhouse is just around the corner."

"Stay a few steps behind me. When we spot the white Toyota, just follow my lead."

"Copy."

John pulled into a parking space on the street. Xander exited the SUV and began walking down the sidewalk. The street was lined with townhouses on both sides. It looked to be a very affluent part of town. They were all three stories, as far as he could tell, connected to each other on both sides. The neighbors in the surrounding homes were all blissfully unaware that the nightmare they were watching on television was being controlled by someone right next-door. The people walking by, on their way to dinner or to the White House to see what was going on, hadn't a clue either.

War was different than it used to be. Technology had made it possible to fight from anywhere, even the comfort of your own living room—or, in Anastasia's case, the living room of some poor homeowner who was quite possibly already dead.

The evening was starting to cool. The street lamps had just come on. Xander could feel the weight of his Glock 19 at the small of his back. He could feel the slight bulge of his knife in his left pocket. As he walked down the street, he scanned, and up ahead he saw the white Toyota Camry. It was across the street, but directly in front of the townhouse. He slid his hand in his pocket and gripped his knife. Xander glanced over his shoulder. John was crossing the street to his side, giving a nod in the Camry's direction. They were on the same page. That would be critical over the next ten minutes.

Xander never liked working with anyone new. Not on a life-or-death mission. But a combat Marine was a different story. John would know all the ins and outs of following directions. There would be no ad-libbing. That wasn't how they were trained.

Xander patted on his right hip. Out of the corner of his eye he saw John turn for the Camry's passenger-side door. They were in sync. Xander smiled widely and walked right up to the driver-side window and gave it a knock. The man behind the wheel gave him a scowl, and Xander heard him say a muffled "get lost."

Xander scrunched his nose and held up his index finger, as if to say, "I just have a quick question".

John was about to reach the trunk of the Camry. The driver glanced over to his partner beside him, then back to Xander, rolled his eyes, and made the terrible mistake of rolling down the window. From what Marvin said about the Camry, they weren't sure that these two thirty-something men were security for Anastasia as she was working away in the townhouse. But when

Xander watched the man slide his right hand around the grip of a pistol in between his seat and the car's console, it was clear they weren't there to take their niece on a chaperoned date to the movies. Xander thumbed the blade of his knife open down by his left side.

"Get lost, buddy, I'm not going to tell you again," the man said as his window finished opening.

"I'm sorry, just a quick question."

Xander watched out of his periphery as John walked up beside the passenger window and pulled his pistol.

"Can you tell me which way to stop a terrorist?"

The man had no chance to register what Xander said before Xander plunged the knife through the front of his neck. As the passenger scrambled for his weapon, John tapped on his window, and when the man saw the gun trained on his head, he put both hands up in surrender.

"Get out of the car," Xander told him. The driver clutched at his neck, but he was already growing weak.

A few people were walking toward Xander on the sidewalk. Xander pulled his gun and held it on the passenger as he exited the Camry. After John patted down the man, Xander nodded John toward the civilians walking their way. John put his gun away, walked over to them, showed his CIA credentials, and turned them in the opposite direction.

"Hands on the car where I can see them," Xander told the man.

"Look, I don't know what the hell is going on here. I was just hired to stop anyone from going inside the townhouse. I don't even know that asshole." He motioned toward the driver who was now slumped over dead.

"What townhouse?" Xander wanted to confirm.

The man glanced over his shoulder at the same townhouse Dbie had sent him to.

"How many are inside?"

"I told you, I don't know anything. When I got here, two men gave us half our money. Told us we get the other half in the morning."

"Were they American?" Xander asked.

"No. They looked like they were from the Middle East. I don't know, man. Please, just don't kill me. I'm just a security guard trying to make some extra cash."

Xander believed him.

"If I see you again tonight, you will die. Understood?"

The man glanced back inside the car where the driver was still very much dead. Then he looked back up at Xander.

"I understand."

John's phone began to vibrate in Xander's pocket.

Xander asked, "What's your name?"

"Eric."

"Eric, leave your phone on the hood of the car and get lost."

The man did as Xander asked and sprinted down the street.

Xander ducked down behind the Camry and answered the phone.

"This is Xander."

"Xander, it's Director Hartsfield. Marvin said you needed to speak with me?"

Xander let out a long sigh, then moved aside to make sure Agent Karn wasn't near enough to hear him.

"Are you alone, Mary?"

"I can be. Just one second."

Xander heard some shuffling and a door close.

"All right, what is it? What can I do?"

Xander asked, "This line is secure?"

"Yes, Xander, you're scaring me. What is it?"

Xander only had one word for Mary. A word he hoped he would never have to say, yet here he was.

"Phoenix."

49

Time to Cut the Power

Director Hartsfield was quiet. Apparently it was a word she never expected to hear either.

"Mary, I don't have time for this to be a thing. I just need to know that you heard me."

"I heard you, Xander, but I have to ask . . . You're certain about this?"

"It's the only way," Xander said without hesitation.

Mary let out a sigh. "I will get everything prepared."

"Thank you. I am going to stop Anastasia and end this thing. Then I'll be in touch."

"Good luck, Xander."

Xander ended the call. John finished turning a few more people in the opposite direction, then came over to Xander as he dialed Marvin.

Marv answered quickly. "Nice work on the Camry."

"What does the other side of this townhouse look like?"

"Small courtyard, French doors leading out to a patio."

Xander ended the call.

"John, go around back. I'm going through the front door. Don't let anyone escape in your direction."

"Copy that. Any idea what's waiting inside?"

"No."

John nodded.

"Mind if I hang on to your phone?"

"Of course not. Be careful, sir."

"I'll see you on the other side," Xander said.

John left his side and made his way down the street to get to the back side of the townhouse. Xander couldn't shake the feeling of impending doom. Maybe it was because the White House was currently under attack. Or maybe it was the fact that everyone he loved had been targeted by Anastasia Maragos, aka the Greek Muslim extremist. He had no idea how deep her organization was, but it was clearly deeper than her brothers and a United States congressman. Even if he got to Anastasia before she could push the button herself, he believed her when she said she had a plan in place to make sure Xander would comply or his loved ones would die.

He needed to stop Anastasia from harming anyone else. He stood up from the side of the Camry, rolled the window up so no one would see the dead man inside, then walked across the street to the front door.

He texted Marv.

Cut the power in twenty seconds.

Marv replied, *Copy that.*

Xander tucked his Glock at the small of his back, but kept his knife ready down by his side. He knocked on the front door.

"We don't want any, thank you," a man responded from behind the door.

"It's Eric," Xander said. "A suspicious man just walked around back. I think there's trouble."

The door jerked open, and Xander plunged his knife into the man's throat, ensuring that he couldn't scream. The man gargled blood as Xander let him down quietly to the floor.

"Who was it?" a man called from the other room.

There was a living room just to Xander's left. He quickly dragged the body of the dying man in there with him. Eric was right, they were Middle Eastern.

"Umarah?" The man called for his partner again. "Who the hell was at the door? And what happened to the power?"

The man was moving closer; it sounded like he was in the hallway now. Xander let go of the dead man, took back his knife, and inched forward, putting his back against the wall beside the open doorway to the hall. The front door was still ajar. Xander looked down and saw some of the man's blood pooled on the marble floor at the entrance. He readied his knife in his right hand.

"Umarah?"

"Everything all right down there?" Xander heard a woman shout from upstairs.

Anastasia.

"Everything is fine. Don't worry. I will have the power back on in seconds," the man answered.

He was walking down the hallway now, which Xander could tell by how his voice echoed. A second later, he could see the man's shadow come into view. Xander tightened his grip on the knife.

"Sharifu, check the perimeter in back," the man said.

There were at least two more men. The man coming down the hall, and Sharifu, the man he just ordered to check the perimeter. That knowledge was a lucky break. Xander fully intended to make the most of it. For now, the shadow was moving closer. The man would see the blood in front of the door any second now. Xander had to make sure he got to him before he was able to alert anyone. Especially Anastasia. If she felt as though she were in danger, she might do something rash and kill one or all of his loved ones. A pang of worry zapped Xander's gut. He swallowed hard and focused.

One thing at a time.

When the man noticed the blood, things happened fast. Xander heard the man's footsteps on the marble in the hallway turn into a jog, then squeak to a stop. Xander rounded the wall and stabbed at the man's neck, but the man had already begun to move to check the door and was able to jerk back just in time as the blade of Xander's knife hit nothing but air. The man grabbed Xander under the armpits and pushed him backward carrying him back into the living room and falling on top of him. This man was big and strong; Xander would have to best him with speed and technique.

"What's going on down there?" Anastasia shouted from upstairs.

The man pinned Xander's knife hand against the carpet and was getting ready to answer Anastasia. If he did, it could be a disaster. Xander quickly jabbed the man's throat with his left hand, stopping him just before he shouted. He then wrapped his legs around the man, and his left arm around his head, and pulled him into him. The man fought against Xander's squeeze, but for the moment, he was able to keep the man from rising. He could hear him wheezing as Xander did his best to bury his mouth against his chest to keep what noise he did make muffled.

"Yazid! Answer me. What is going on down there. I can't afford *any* interruptions!"

Xander only had a few seconds before she was going to investigate. He had to end this now. He continued to squeeze with all his might to hold Yazid in place. But he needed to get his other hand free. The man's grip was strong, but the blade of the knife was long enough that Xander could turn it downward in his fingers and start to press it into the man's hand. When he did, the man began to groan. Xander let go of his head and punched several times at his throat. With the light off in the room he couldn't really see. The knife was digging in the man far enough now, forcing him to let go.

"Yazid!"

Xander could hear footfalls on the stairs.

Anastasia was coming.

Time was up.

50

Weapons of Minimal Destruction?

YAZID FINALLY REGAINED his wits enough to raise up on Xander and draw back his arm to bring down a punch. This put him off balance enough that Xander was able to bridge his hips upward and roll the big man over onto his back. Yazid was caught off guard by the move and never recovered. Xander slid the blade of his knife in the right side of Yazid's neck, and the struggle stopped underneath him. Unfortunately for Xander, the damage to his cover was already done. When he turned to get up off the dead man, Anastasia came running around the corner.

For a moment, they both just stared at each other. She was in shock, and Xander was calculating what to do next.

Instinct made him reach for the gun at the small of his back. Instinct made her dart back down the hallway for the stairs. Xander knew that if she made it to her computer, she could engage the nanochips that were inside of his loved ones.

"Stop!" Xander shouted as he sprinted forward.

He had to beat her to her computer. Or at least keep her from getting there. As he took his first step into the hallway, he simultaneously saw her at the foot of the stairs and raised his gun to shoot.

He had her.

But just as he squeezed the trigger, his foot slid out from under him and the bullet flew off line into the wall. Xander's body slammed against the foyer table. The blood of the man who'd answered the door had made him slip, possibly costing him the lives of everyone he loved. He recovered as quickly as he could, sliding once more before he regained traction and ran for the stairs. He leapt up the first four, then one more stride up the next four, then he dove to the top, his gun extended in front of him.

It was too late.

Anastasia was behind the couch, only her laptop visible, resting on top of a cushion. The wall of windows behind her showed her reflection; she was typing away as fast as she could.

"I'll shoot you through the couch, Anastasia. Stop typing!"

There was great desperation in Xander's voice.

There was not in Anastasia's. "If you miss, though, they are all dead."

"You can't make it out of this, Anastasia." He rose to his feet, not moving his aim from where she sat behind the couch. "I have a man downstairs. I have the CIA watching the townhouse right now."

"I told you, Xander, it doesn't matter if I make it out of this or not. I am not the only one involved in this. My partner is ready with the next step in the plan. So if you don't hold up your end of the bargain—"

Anastasia was interrupted by the sound of gunshots in the backyard. Xander was about to make a move when the wall of windows behind Anastasia shattered and the report of the gunshots that blasted them reached his ears. The laptop Anastasia was holding fell forward onto the couch. Xander jumped the ottoman, took the computer in his hands, and peered over the couch. Anastasia had been fatally wounded. She was slumped, folded in half, dead.

Xander looked out the glassless window, and Agent Karn stood below him holding his gun.

"Secure the house," Xander told him.

"Copy. Xander, I shot her because she had a gun," John said.

Xander looked back down, and sure enough, under her right leg lay a pistol.

"Good work, now secure the house."

John nodded and walked forward.

Xander wasn't sure how to feel. On one hand, for now, his friends were safe. But if word got out that Anastasia was dead before he could hold up his end of the deal they made on the phone, his loved ones could still be in danger. According to her, her "partner" was waiting with specific protocol. Xander and John may have just ensured the safety of the people at the White House, but nothing had changed for Sam, Kyle, Sarah, and his sister, Helen.

The people at the White House.

Xander once again stopped his pity party short, pulled his cell phone, and dialed the plane. Dbie picked up on the first ring.

She was frantic. "They are in the White House. I can't stop them!"

"Yes you can, Dbie."

"What?"

Xander pulled the laptop open in front of him. What he was looking at was like a video game screen, and it may as well have been Chinese. He knew there was no time to get the laptop to Dbie, so he had to bring Dbie to the laptop.

"Tell Bob I'm going to FaceTime his cell phone. I have Anastasia's laptop and I need you to tell me how to shut these things down."

"Where is Anastasia?"

"Don't worry about that, Dbie. If I can show you the screen on FaceTime, will you be able to walk me through how to shut them down?"

"Y-yes. Yes, but hurry!"

Xander ended the call and started a video call with Bob's phone. Dbie answered on the first ring again. The next fifteen minutes were nearly impossible for Xander to follow, but somehow Dbie had managed to get him to press all the right buttons. Xander watched on-screen as the nanobots' cameras showed them going from flying around the White House to landing harmlessly on the ground.

"You got them all?" Xander said.

"That's all of them. You did it, Xander. You stopped her."

"You did, Dbie. Thank you. I'll call you if I need anything else. For now, though, the bourbon is under the sink. Bob can help you if you need it."

The moment Xander ended the call, Anastasia's computer went black.

"Dead battery?" John asked from beside Xander.

"No, the battery was just at 75 percent."

Xander knew before even checking that Anastasia's phone would be wiped as well. He walked over, found it in her pocket, and sure enough, it was completely fried. Xander didn't have to know much about technology to know that the partner Anastasia spoke of was working on closing her out. They wouldn't know that she was dead, but they would have seen that she stopped manipulating the nanobots. Xander's worst fears were confirmed in that moment. If he didn't follow through with what Anastasia demanded of him, his loved ones would all be dead.

"Is it dead too?" John said.

For a second, Xander didn't know what John meant, he was so much in his own head. Then he looked down at Anastasia's phone and nodded. He dialed Marvin.

"You okay, X? The drone is almost there."

"I'm good. We don't need the drone. Dbie and I just got all of the nanobots offline."

"What? Already?"

"Anastasia Maragos is dead. We used her laptop to shut them down. But Marv, let's keep this Anastasia thing on total lockdown until we know more about who she's working with."

"Of course. I'll send a cleanup crew."

"Call Brandon Sizemore and tell him to evacuate the White House right now. The bots are inactive, but we don't know for certain whether or not her American helper, Jerry McDonnell, can reactivate them somehow. So get them out of there now."

"I'm on it. Jerry McDonnell, Xander?"

"Yeah. It will make more sense soon. Get a team to his home as well. Full search. I don't care what hoops you have to jump through, it needs to happen fast."

"Copy. You coming in?"

"I'm going to see my team."

"Check in with Director Hartsfield if you don't mind. She has been a nervous wreck since you last spoke with her."

"I'll call her on my way." Xander ended the call.

"Well, that went about as good as it could have," John said.

In a way he was right, but Xander had more of the story.

"It did," Xander said. "You mind sticking around and making sure the cleanup crew has all the information they need? I have to go see my team at the hospital."

"I'll take care of everything. Here's the keys to the Suburban."

John tossed the keys to Xander. Xander walked over to where John stood. They saluted each other, then exchanged a heartfelt handshake.

"Thanks for your help tonight, John. I'll make sure Director Hartsfield knows you were the one who saved the White House."

"You don't have to do that, sir. You were the one that shut down the bots."

Xander nodded. "Mind if I hang on to your phone a little longer?"

"No problem."

Xander gave a halfhearted smile and started down the stairs. Before he stepped around the blood on the floor that almost ruined the entire night, he set the keys to John's SUV on the table by the front door. He wouldn't be needing them. All he wanted to do was talk to his loved ones, make sure they were all okay. But he had to call the director of the CIA first.

51

Phoenix

Xander flipped through the radio stations on the Toyota Camry's dashboard. It was too quiet in the car, and he needed to fill the air with something.

"In the mood for anything in particular?" Xander asked the dead man with the hole in his throat that he had moved over into the passenger seat when he took the Camry. "No?" Apparently, the guy was in no mood to talk.

Xander fiddled a little more with the radio and stopped when he heard Ray Lamontagne's husky vocals fill up the car completely. Ray had always been one of Xander's favorites, but it was extra meaningful that the song he was singing was "Let It Be Me." He belted the chorus, singing about friendship, in a way that only Ray can. Xander had always done his best to be a good friend. And even though what he was about to do was for the sake of his friends, he couldn't help but think about the fact that they wouldn't be in their current predicament if it wasn't for him.

He turned off Constitution Avenue onto Virginia Avenue, just Xander and his lifeless passenger. It had been about fifteen minutes since he ended his call with CIA Director Mary Hartsfield. He was thankful she had everything in place. He made a loop around the White House just to see the hoopla in person. Of course he couldn't get close enough to see much detail. The military had moved in by that point, keeping everyone at bay.

All Xander wanted now was to talk to his friends. He had called his sister as soon as he hung up with Mary. She was doing fine. He didn't ask her about a mosquito bite. He didn't want to scare her. But he knew it had happened. Anastasia Maragos hadn't lied about anything else. There wasn't anything anyone could do for his sister anyway. He just hoped his deal with Anastasia was enough to save her. To save them all. He knew in the back of his mind that if Anastasia did have a partner with a plan in place, it wouldn't be long before they called, threatening the same thing Anastasia had. Xander just hoped he could find the partner before he could do irreparable damage. He would start with Jerry McDonnell. That is, if Marv and crew hadn't already taken care of him.

Only time would tell.

Up ahead, a part of the Potomac River branched off and came up alongside the road. Rock Creek, he thought it was called. Somewhere in there was a turn to the hospital. There was also a bridge to a small marina he had been to once before. The turn came up on him sooner than expected. He must have gotten lost in the music. He quickly took out John's phone and called Sam. In the rearview mirror, he saw a car's headlights swerve around a couple other vehicles; it was coming up on him fast.

Sam's phone rang for a third time.

"Come on, Sam. Pick up!" he shouted.

She didn't. It went to voice mail. The car behind him was speeding right up on his ass. It was clear it wasn't going to stop. Xander swerved and made a quick left under the overpass and continued down Virginia. He could see the bridge to the marina up ahead. Just then John's phone began to ring.

"Sam!"

"Sorry, we were having some tests run and—"

"Phoenix!" It was all he had time for.

He glanced once more in his rearview mirror, and the car coming fast slammed into the back of the Camry. He was almost to the bridge, but with his car careening off the road, there was no way he was going to make it.

"What, Xander? You can't be serious! Is this a joke?" Sam was scared and shocked, but Xander had no time to explain. He jerked the steering wheel hard to his left, but the car slammed into the back of him again.

"Phoenix, Sam. Phoenix!"

He dropped the phone as he gripped the steering wheel with both hands. Rock Creek was coming fast. The car behind him slammed into him once again, harder this time, and the Camry rocketed toward the water. He slammed on the brakes, but the nose of the car had already slid over the embankment. The water came at the front window with astonishing speed. Then there was a violent splash.

The seat belt jerked hard, and Xander's head jerked forward. His forearms burned from the impact with the airbag. Somehow he'd managed to keep his wits. Everything was quiet now. All he could hear was his own heavy breathing and the sound of the Camry rocking in the water. It began to pitch its hood down into the cold inlet. Xander unlatched his seat belt. The water was beginning to make its way inside the car. If he didn't get out fast, he was going to drown. He tried the door, but it wouldn't open. The driver-side window was now completely submerged. Everything was turning dark.

The Camry's back end was pitching further and further. The car was half-submerged now. He pulled his knife from his pocket and placed the stainless steel bearing at the bottom against the middle of the window, smacked the top of the closed knife with his right palm as hard as he could, and the window cracked. He leaned over with his back on the middle console and kicked the window out with his left foot. As the creek rushed inside like a waterfall, Xander glanced back through the rear window. It was now facing skyward, and the only thing in view was the top of the creek bed.

The man standing on top of the creek bed glowed red in the taillights of Xander's sinking vehicle. The dark sky stood in contrast behind him, making it easy to notice he was holding something up on his shoulder.

He was holding an RPG.

And the grenade's tip was unmistakably pointed right at Xander.

52

Fallen

THE SUN CAME up over Washington, DC. By all accounts, it was going to be a beautiful spring day. Most of DC was celebrating the fact that the President was alive and the terrorist attack had been thwarted by the power of the US military and its agencies.

Most of DC.

At the hospital where Team Reign had been taken for observation, in a top secret room to keep their identities hidden, there was no celebration at all.

The exact opposite.

None of them believed what Sam had told them. She turned on the television to prove it. A female reporter sat at her anchor desk and spoke solemnly into the camera:

Good morning again, DC. Breaking news at this hour.

In a square graphic that hovered over the reporter's right shoulder, the words *Breaking News* disappeared, replaced by a headshot picture of Xander King, smiling big for the camera. It was taken at the Kentucky Derby.

Sarah gasped in the seat next to Kyle.

Kyle began to sob. "No. No-no-no-no!"

The reporter continued with the story:

As if there wasn't enough terrible news to report out of the nation's capitol today, we have another tragic story. Kentucky Derby–winning horseman, bourbon entrepreneur, and veteran Navy SEAL Alexander King was found dead early this morning. He apparently lost control of his vehicle after missing his turn onto the highway, skidded out of control, slammed against the underpass, igniting an explosion in the car. The car continued down into Rock Creek where an eyewitness said it was a ball of flames by the time it hit the water. Alexander is survived by his sister and his niece. The horse racing world will be devastated by the loss. We offer our condolences to his family and friends.

In other news the President will hold a press conference on the south lawn of the—

Sam turned off the television. It had been a long night for her especially, and she was exhausted. She still couldn't believe how things turned out.

"This isn't real. This can't be happening." Kyle was up and pacing the room. His world was turned upside down. Sam knew that Xander was much more than a friend. They were brothers. Sam had long felt the same about Xander. All of it was beyond heartbreaking.

"What the hell do we do? What about his sister? His horses? His . . . everything? He can't be gone!"

Sam wiped the tears from her eyes and cleared her throat. "Xander was prepared for a day like this, Kyle. The two of us spoke of it often. He left strict instructions for everything. You don't have to worry about any of it."

"Yeah? Well, what about us? What are we supposed to do? I don't want to live a life without him."

Kyle buried his head in his hands. He was completely shattered.

Sam tried to be positive. "You know Xander would want you to live on and be happy. You know that, Kyle."

Kyle picked up the chair beside him and flung it against the concrete block wall. It shattered into a dozen pieces. Sam looked over at Sarah crying into her hands and imagined all of their hearts were shattered in much the same way. Jack and Zhanna had similar reactions when she talked to them on the phone a few moments ago. They were recovering in a hospital just outside of CIA headquarters. This news would only make their recovery more difficult.

Sam wanted to comfort Kyle, but she knew it was no use. They were all devastated. Words, no matter how poignant, would fall flat.

News of how Xander and John Karn handled Anastasia Maragos at the townhouse had made its way to Sam as well. She never doubted for a minute that they would be able to stop Anastasia. They were all incredibly lucky that Dbie Johnson had been hired into the Maragos' operation. That had probably been the Maragos' biggest mistake. She almost singlehandedly saved hundreds, maybe thousands of lives.

With the news of how Anastasia had been brought down, they also received news of what exactly had been injected into them. The fact that at any moment the chips inside all of them, including Xander's sister, could be triggered, and they could all die, was terrifying. But all of them took it in stride. There was nothing they could do about it at the moment. Marvin and the CIA's finest were putting together a team to find a way to find the chips and remove them, if that was possible. In the meantime, they all agreed to let go of what they couldn't control and not let it bother them. Sam knew some of them would deal better with that than others.

All arrangements for Xander's funeral were laid out in his

will. He had designated people to take care of every detail, Xander's last effort to make sure he took care of everyone. Even after he was gone.

FBI discovered Xander was right about Congressman Jerry McDonnell helping with the money and materials for the nanobots. Seems as though Anastasia had already been through needing him, however. When FBI went to search his home, they found him and his wife dead in their beds. The only sign of foul play were tiny mosquito-like bites on their necks. The FBI found a cell phone in Jerry's bag that had been communicating with Greece for a long time. A loose end tied off.

Andonios Maragos was the only family member left. Marvin had tracked him to London where they would no doubt soon find him, then determine to what level he was involved.

The rest was a nightmare Sam wished she could wake up from. But she was all too familiar with these sorts of nightmares. The ones that never go away. As she looked at the hurt on the faces of the only people in the world that she truly cared about, she hoped that one day this pain would subside.

She wasn't going to hold her breath.

Sam felt more alone in that moment than she ever had in her life. Xander had been the only constant in her life over the last several years. He'd been a brother, a friend, a partner in crime, and quite honestly . . . the love of her life. *Nothing* would be the same without him. She had no idea what was next. But she was already itching for a fight. She had no intentions of stopping the work that brought her and Xander so close in the first place. If for no other reason, she would do it for him.

53

The Visit

Senator Graham Thomas pulled into his garage, slid out of his car, and walked into his house. He was finally home. It had been an excruciatingly long day on Capitol Hill. Hour after hour of safety meetings, security briefings, interviews, listening to never-ending horror stories, and all he wanted to do was get home and have a drink.

A celebratory drink.

Though the day wasn't a total win, he was still winning. President Williams surviving the attack wasn't best-case scenario. But once the sting of not getting his revenge passed, Graham was able to see that it didn't really matter. He had the last laugh. The money he would make from the nanobot technology would far surpass what he lost when the President abruptly shut down Everworld. Bonus now was that he wouldn't have to deal with Anastasia Maragos. Turns out it was a good thing Xander King had survived the attempts Brancati made on his life after all.

Graham got what he wanted out of all this, and King killing Anastasia, the poor bastard's last accomplishment on Earth, actually gave Graham an easier route to all his riches.

It all worked out in the end.

Though Graham didn't know for certain that it was Xander who killed Anastasia, it was the only logical conclusion. King would have been the only one to know about her. It was the very reason Graham tied Rig's Recycling in Greece to Anastasia in the first place—the trail would lead right to her, not Graham.

It was time for that celebratory drink.

Graham didn't bother turning on the lights. He walked over to the fireplace, lit a starter log, and threw it atop the wood cradled inside. He delighted in the crackle of the growing yellow-orange flame. It reminded him of the report he'd seen that afternoon, of Alexander King going up in flames. His body so charred, you couldn't even tell it was him. A stark contrast to the handsome picture they'd been showing on television all day long.

"Better you than me, pretty boy," Graham said to the fire.

He watched for a moment longer, then strolled over to the wet bar. He rolled up his sleeves, removed the top on his glass decanter that held his finest scotch whiskey, and poured a few fingers to enjoy by the fire. This entire thing had turned out cleaner than he could ever have hoped. No one, including his old friend Jerry McDonnell, was left alive to pin anything on him.

He took a long sip of his scotch, but before he could swallow, he spit every bit of it out in a fit of shock. From the dark shadows of the connected dining room, a man's voice broke the fire-crackling silence in the room.

"You *almost* got away with it."

Graham dropped his glass, and it shattered on the floor. He backed away from the dining room, toward the fireplace, his eyes desperately searching the darkness to find the owner of the voice.

"Who the hell are you? I've got a shotgun loaded by the bar.

I'm not afraid to use it." Graham tried his best not to reveal his searing fear in his voice.

The man didn't speak again. Graham winced when something came toward him from the darkness, and he jumped when a loud thud echoed in the room. When Graham opened his eyes and looked down, he saw his double-barreled shotgun lying at his feet. The break action open. The gun empty.

The man in the shadows spoke again. His voice was eerily calm. "You mean *that* shotgun?"

A chill ran down Graham's spine. He didn't know who was there in the room with him, but it was clear he was in a lot of trouble.

"What do you want?" Graham was starting to panic. "Who are you? Be a man and show yourself."

Three heavy footsteps headed his way before a tall and muscular man stepped into the light of the fire.

Graham's mouth went slack. His jaw nearly bounced off the floor. He couldn't believe his eyes.

"Xander King?"

Graham finally closed his gaping mouth and shuddered at the man standing before him.

"But . . . But you're . . ."

"Dead?" Xander answered for him. "You sure?"

"I saw the news." Graham was in a state of shock. "I saw— everyone is talking about how you died."

Xander took a step closer. "Senator, tsk-tsk, you of all people should know that you can't believe everything you see on the news."

He took another step forward, and Graham took a step back, shock still etched onto his weathered face. He tried to regain his composure.

"What do you want, King?"

Xander stood stoic.

"That's easy. Justice."

"Justice for what? You think I had something to do with whoever tried to have you killed?"

"No," Xander said, very matter-of-fact, "because *I* had me killed."

Graham shook his head. "I don't know what you're talking about. Maybe you should get to the hospital or something. I can drive you."

Xander pulled something from his pocket. Graham recoiled in fear. But when he saw it was the vial from his wet bar in Xander's hand, he just looked on without speaking.

Xander held up the vial. "I was wondering how Alessio Brancati knew every move I was making. What kind of man takes advantage of a woman like that?"

Graham played dumb. "Alessio Brancati? Who the hell is that? And what woman are you talking about? I don't even know what that stuff is." He pointed at the vial.

Xander tossed the vial on the floor next to the shotgun and moved on. "You know what your problem is, Senator Thomas?"

Xander waited for an answer, then continued when Graham remained silent.

"You think you are smarter than everyone else. In fact, men like you *know* you are smarter than everyone else. And that is a serious weakness. You know why?"

Graham was starting to get angry. Who in the hell did this guy think he was? Talking to a United States senator like this. "Sounds like you're about to tell me."

Xander continued, "The reason it's a weakness is because when you start to believe it, that you are always the smartest person in the room, you start to get arrogant. You know what happens when you get cocky, Senator Thomas?"

"You can't touch me, King. You have nothing."

"When you get cocky, you make mistakes. Big mistakes. Mistakes that only an egotistical prick like you would make, and it is the very thing that brings you down in the end."

Graham had no idea what Xander was talking about. Clearly he thought he found something on him, but Graham knew he didn't, because he really was the smartest person in the room. Especially this room.

"There a point to all this, Xander? Or you just like to hear yourself talk?"

"Like I said, you almost got away with it. But Graham, I watched a lot of football with my father when I was growing up. Especially top ten college football. That mean anything to you?"

"Fuck you."

"Yeah, I thought you might say that. See, there was just something about the name of the recycling company in Greece that kept gnawing at me."

Graham's stomach dropped.

"I had some time alone today, you know, being dead and all. And along with combing through the entire situation in my mind, making sure I didn't miss anything, I took the time to go back and look at all the board members of Everworld Solutions. Jerry McDonnell was obvious. Guess that's why he's dead. But when I saw your name, that was when I realized what continued to eat at my gut, and why."

"Is that right?" Graham had nothing else to offer. His nerves were so fried that his insides were close to becoming his outsides.

"That's right. Because I remember watching the national championship game one year when I was a kid. The Texas Long- horns were playing, and they were heavy favorites. One of the reasons they were so heavily favored was because of their defense. A defense headed up by the best linebacker in college football, Graham "Big *Rig*" Thomas. I remember my dad saying you used to hit like a Mack truck." Xander gave a mocking laugh and shook his head.

Graham took another step back. It was time to fight for his life. If he could somehow get the best of Xander here, he was home free. With his shotgun lying empty at his feet, the only thing he could think to do was get to the tools by the fireplace and shove the wrought iron poker right through this arrogant bastard's heart.

"So what of it?" Graham stalled.

"Rig's Recycling. You dumb son of bitch." There was venom in Xander's voice now. "You were so egotistical that you had to leave a mark that you could laugh at later and name the recycling company after your old college football nickname. You thought because you put it in Anastasia's husband's name that no one would ever figure out your little inside joke. Well . . . who's laughing now?"

Graham was almost to the wrought iron poker. "Well, congratulations to you. You win the prize. What are you going to do, Xander? Huh? Turn me in? There is still no trail on me. The name of the recycling company will be seen as a coincidence in the courts."

"I agree," Xander said. He took another step forward.

"So what then? You going to kill me? A United States senator? They fry you for that. They will. Whether you can prove I was in the wrong or not, they will kill you."

Xander grinned a devilish grin. "Graham . . . you can't kill what's already dead."

Graham's blood ran cold. Now he understood what Xander meant a moment ago when he said he had himself killed. If the world thought he was dead, he couldn't be blamed for something like this. It was over for Graham if he didn't do something immediately.

Graham took a long step back and turned toward the fireplace, grabbed the wrought iron poker in his hands, turned back, swinging it as hard as he could, but he was too slow. Xander had already rushed forward; he caught Graham's swinging hands with his own, stopping him from landing his attack. Xander's grip was strong. Too strong. With a quick twist of his arms, Xander managed to get the poker from Graham's grasp and fling it across the room, clanging against the hard-wood floor.

"One chance to get out of this alive," Xander said. "Who else knows about the nanochips in my friends' bloodstream?"

"What?" Graham said. "I don't know what you mean. Your friends? Nanochips?"

"If there is anyone else, I will find them. No matter how long it takes. And because I'm 'dead,' they will never see me coming."

"I really don't know what you're talking about. I swear. But maybe I can help you find what you're looking for." Graham was grasping at straws.

Xander shook his head. "No. You can't. And that's where you made your biggest mistake."

"What? What mistake?"

Xander's devilish grin was gone. "Not being of any use to me."

Graham watched Xander move his arm out of sight, and when it returned, the fire glinted something metal in his hand.

He had no time to protest before the blade was inside of him. The last thing Graham saw before he bled to death on the floor was Xander taking a bottle of bourbon from his bar and walking out the door.

54

Secret Weapon

NOT MANY PEOPLE get to see what the weather is like on the day of their funeral. Then again, not many people lived the crazy life that Alexander King did, so for him it wasn't too much of a surprise. The rain actually made it easier for him to stay hidden. The poncho acted as a good cover. He brought flowers so it would look like he was just another loved one coming to visit a nearby grave. He felt the gray clouds overhead to be more than appropriate. The rain continuing down like tears, mourning his former life.

Meanwhile, about a hundred plots away, a massive crowd of people gathered. Not just Xander's loved ones, acquaintances, and business associates, but a full brigade of former and current military. Though Xander was being buried in a civilian cemetery, it didn't stop them from giving the former Navy SEAL the full treatment. It was a humbling sight to see so many gathered in his honor.

What a strange thing to watch your own funeral. As he stood in front of someone else's headstone, watching the proceedings out of the corner of his eye, he couldn't believe where his life had taken him. Before his father turned on his family on the day his mother was murdered in front of him, the day that changed the course of his life forever, all Xander ever wanted to be was a baseball player. The dream of millions of little boys. He hadn't really considered it much over the last fifteen years, but with the day being what it was, he couldn't help but wonder what his life would be like right then if his dad hadn't turned on them. If he had finished high school like every other kid, would he be playing in ball parks all across the country? One thing was certain, he wouldn't be standing in the rain watching people lower his casket into the ground.

In a way, his life now could be a fresh start. He could go and try to make a life somewhere. A life all his own. Something he'd never had before. He could just disappear to some foreign country, find a beautiful woman, make babies, and live out the rest of his days as a normal human being. He could, but that just wasn't who he was now. Regardless of the chain of events that led him to being a soldier, there was no denying it was what he was meant to be. There would never be anything in life he was better at. And now that he'd had a taste for the adrenaline of bringing someone to justice, even a home run to win the World Series wouldn't make him feel alive in the same way. Not even close.

But even though he wouldn't be leaving to find a life of romance, he still planned to disappear. There were only two people on planet Earth who knew Xander was still alive. He had the foresight years ago to know that a situation like this could be on the horizon. Calling both Mary Hartsfield and Sam Harrison and announcing the code word *Phoenix* meant an entire protocol went into action. Sam went to work making sure he had everything he needed to disappear. Clothes, cash, passports, and a host of other things for the months to come. For Mary Hartsfield it meant setting up his death, making it look to the world as though he were truly dead. This was why Xander took the Toyota Camry with the dead man inside from the townhouse. Mary would make sure that the man in the car would be identified as Xander, giving his loved ones a body to grieve over and his potential enemies evidence that the war hero was gone for good.

The past couple days had been hard for Xander. But he imagined they were even harder for his sister and his niece, for Kyle and Sarah, and everyone else he was close to. Even Sam. Though she knew he was alive, she might never see him again. As cruel as it seemed to make them all believe he was dead, he knew it was a case of being cruel to be kind. He was saving their lives by disappearing. It was going to be the hardest thing he'd ever done. But there was no other way. He had given them a chance to continue to live and find happiness. And that was all that mattered to Xander. And now that phase one of *Phoenix* was wrapping up a few headstones over, it was time to move into phase two.

Now that Xander was "dead," he could truly move through the world like a ghost. A real-life secret weapon. This was the other reason Director Hartsfield needed to know he was going to stage his death. She could use him to move chess pieces in the world of warfare that would save countless lives. Xander's sole purpose for living now. And with Sam continuing as his handler, the sky was the limit. In his will he had given her full control of his money and assets. She could appropriate it to whoever needed it. And she would be able to help Xander move in the shadows while keeping him equipped with everything he would ever need to have an advantage over his enemy. Whoever that enemy may be.

Xander felt as good as he could about his current situation. He felt as though his loved ones were most likely in the clear. Now that Anastasia, Jerry McDonnell, and Senator Graham Thomas were all dead, the only one left in the equation was Andonios Maragos. But based on what Sarah had said about him, he didn't believe Andonios had been very involved. Be certain, though: Xander would find out for sure.

All in all, Xander felt the life-threatening nanochips injected by the nanobots would lie dormant in his friends until they figured out how to find and remove them. Regardless, because of how adamant Anastasia was that Xander disappear, that if he didn't, her so-called associates would kill his loved ones, he had had no other choice but to do what he did. "Dying," per Anastasia's demand, was the only way he could be certain they would be safe until he knew beyond the shadow of a doubt that it was over.

Xander left the grave he was pretending to peer over and moved a little closer to the people gathered for him. There was a large oak tree not too far from the back of the massive crowd, and he stood behind it to take it all in. He could see that they had begun to fold the flag atop his casket, while a single bugle playing "Taps" was the haunting sound track. Xander's emotion swelled. He was going to miss his life with his loved ones. They were everything to him, which is why a life alone was worth it to see them live on. He could feel the hurt they were feeling deep inside him. He would store that pain away and use it when he needed it most. This was undoubtedly going to change him as a man. He was not necessarily eager to see how, but he knew that it would.

Xander backed away from the tree. Using the binoculars Sam had left him in his go bag, he took one last look at the pain on his niece's and sister's faces. On Kyle's face. On Sarah's, Sam's, and even Natalie Rockwell's faces too. He felt their love, and he would use that as fuel as well. To do what needed to be done in the world. What he was born to do. He couldn't watch them suffer any longer. He put the binoculars down and walked away from his funeral. This might be the last time he ever saw them. He hoped not, but there was just no way to know.

Xander got in a rental car and drove past his house in Lexington one last time. He took one last drive through the rolling hills of his home, taking it all in, as it might be the last time he ever saw it as well. He wasn't sure what was next, but he had become adept at turning the page after tragedy. This would be no different. The life he was born to lead unfortunately didn't afford him any more time with the things and people he loved. And he was okay with that. As long as he could still make a difference . . .

For his family.

For his friends.

For his country.

As Xander drove away from Lexington, Kentucky, away from all that he had ever known and loved . . . toward the great unknown of the future . . .

As he looked down at his new passport that displayed his familiar face beside an unfamiliar name . . . there were a lot of unknowns swirling around him. However, two things had become very clear.

The first thing he knew, which 99.9 percent of the world fortunately didn't know, was a good thing:

He is alive and well.

And though he *is* actually alive and well, the second thing he also knew for certain was an even harder pill to swallow. As everything he ever loved moved further and further away in his rearview mirror, he was left staring straight ahead into the cold eyes of a life entirely alone. And that is when it finally sank in:

He *is* alive and well . . . but Xander King is dead.

WHEN THE MAN COMES AROUND

Ready for something different while you wait for the next Xander King adventure? Order your copy of the first book in Bradley Wright's explosive new Lawson Raines series today!

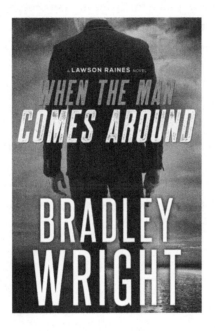

Order your copy from Amazon today!

Former FBI rising star, Lawson Raines, isn't the man he used to be. He's become a monster. Losing your wife, your daughter, and spending ten years behind bars will do that to a man. Especially an innocent one ...

———————————————

"Best book ever. I could not put it down!" - Maryellen Geiger

---

Now Lawson's life sentence has been pardoned, and the people who conspired to put him away are desperately scrambling to bury their little secret in the Las Vegas desert once and for all.

Dodging bullets while chasing clues, Lawson races to uncover the truth behind the conspiracy against him. Along the way, friends become enemies, enemies become friends, and a broken man realizes that his only path to redemption, is revenge. But that path is paved with powerful people--dangerous people. People who took everything from him. And if Lawson can evade their pursuit long enough to find them, he'll prove that a man with nothing to lose might just be the most dangerous of them all.

Order your copy from Amazon today!

ACKNOWLEDGMENTS

First and foremost, I want to thank you, the reader. I love what I do, and no matter how many people help me along the way, none of it would be possible if you weren't turning the pages.

To my family and friends. Thank you for always being there with mountains of support. You all make it easy to dream, and those dreams are what make it into these books. Without you, no fun would be had, much less novels be written.

To my editor, Deb Hall. Thank you for continuing to turn my poorly constructed sentences into a readable story. You are great at what you do, and my work is better for it.

To my advanced reader team. You continue to help make everything I do better. You all have become friends, and I thank you for catching those last few sneaky typos, and always letting me know when something isn't good enough. Xander appreciates you, and so do I.

And finally, to the man or woman who rolled that first cigar. Lifetimes later our puffs of celebration produce clouds of thanks in your honor. Your memory lives on in every stick we light, and every final ash.

About the Author

Bradley Wright is the international bestselling author of action-thrillers. Scourge is his sixth novel. Bradley lives with his family in Lexington, Kentucky. He has always been a fan of great stories, whether it be a song, a movie, a novel, or a binge-worthy television series. Bradley loves interacting with readers on Facebook, Twitter, and via email.

Join the online family:

www.bradleywrightauthor.com
info@bradleywrightauthor.com

Made in the USA
Coppell, TX
01 July 2021

58416948R00166